Mike Cutler.

Gina tried to roll over and push herself up, but she couldn't seem to get her arm beneath her. The snow and clouds and black running shoes all swirled together inside her head.

"Easy, Gina. I need you to lie still. An ambulance is on its way. You've injured your shoulder. I don't want you to aggravate it. And if that bullet is still inside you, I don't want it traveling anywhere." His warm hand cupped her face and she realized just how cold she was. She wished she could wrap her whole body up in that kind of heat. She looked up into his stern expression. "Stay with me."

"Catnip."

"What?"

Her eyelids drifted shut.

"Gina!"

The last thing she saw was her blood seeping into the snow. The last thing she felt was the man's strong hands pressing against her breast and shoulder. The last thing she heard was his voice on her radio.

"Officer down. I repeat, officer down!"

KANSAS CITY COP

USA TODAY Bestselling Author

JULIE MILLER

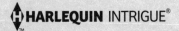

HARLEQUIN INTRIGUE®

To Edna Castillo, reader and bookseller extraordinaire.

A fellow *The Wizard of Oz* fan, too!

Thanks for your help with the Spanish.

Any mistakes are my own.

ISBN-13: 978-1-335-63902-8

Kansas City Cop

Copyright © 2018 by Julie Miller

Recycling programs for this product may not exist in your area.

Printed in U.S.A.

www.Harlequin.com

Julie Miller is an award-winning *USA TODAY* bestselling author of breathtaking romantic suspense—with a National Readers' Choice Award and a Daphne du Maurier Award, among other prizes. She has also earned an *RT Book Reviews* Career Achievement Award. For a complete list of her books, monthly newsletter and more, go to juliemiller.org.

Visit the Author Profile page at Harlequin.com.

CAST OF CHARACTERS

Mike Cutler, Jr.—A second-generation hero with a penchant for rescuing damsels in distress. Having barely survived a tragic childhood, this stubborn, do-the-right-thing physical therapist might not have followed in his father's footsteps to become a cop—but that doesn't mean he isn't all about saving people. Stopping to help a wounded police officer will change his life in ways he never expected. It'll change his heart, too.

Officer Gina Galvan—This tough, working-class cop is the last woman who needs rescuing. But when a life-changing injury jeopardizes her future with KCPD, she turns to Mike Cutler to get her back into fighting shape. Although she's attracted to Mike's blue-eyed charm and tall, fit dependability, she can't see any future for two people who come from such different worlds. But someone out there isn't done hunting cops. And when the shooter targets Gina again, intent on finishing the job he started, she finds much more than an ally in Mike—she finds her very own hero.

Derek Johnson—Gina's partner. Is one of them the shooter's real target? Or is any officer in uniform fair game?

Harold Johnson—Derek's father is an embarrassment to his son.

Lupe and Rollo Molina—Gina's elderly great-aunt and uncle raised her and her siblings.

Sylvie Galvan—Gina's younger sister. She's the pretty one. And that gets her into trouble.

Javier Galvan—Gina's brother used to run with a gang.

Bobby Estes—The creeper boyfriend who won't leave Gina's sister alone.

Gordon and Vicki Bismarck—Ex-husband and wife. No cop wants to answer their domestic violence calls.

Denny Bismarck—Gordon's equally violent big brother leads a motorcycle gang...and protects the family.

Michael Cutler, Sr.—Mike's father, captain of the special weapons and tactics division at KCPD.

Chapter One

The bright sunlight glaring off the fresh February snow through the police cruiser's windshield was as blinding as the headache forming behind Officer Gina Galvan's dark brown eyes.

"No, Tia Mami, I can't." She glanced across the front seat to her partner, Derek Johnson, and silently mouthed an apology for yet another family crisis infringing on their shift time with KCPD. "I don't get off until seven. And that's if our paperwork's done. That's why I left my car at home and took the bus this morning—so Sylvie could drive you and Tio Papi to his doctor's appointment."

"Sylvie no come home from school," her great-aunt Lupe replied quietly, as though apologizing for the news.

"What? Where is she?"

"Javi said he saw her riding with that boyfriend of hers we don't like."

"Seriously?" Anger and concern flooded Gina's cheeks with heat. The boyfriend they didn't like had too much money to have gotten it in the old neighborhood by any legal means. But Bobby Estes's flashy cars and devilish good looks were too much for Gina's dreamy, dissatisfied baby sister to resist. And if Bobby was a teenager, as he claimed, then Gina was Santa Claus. Clearly, her last conversation with Sylvie, about the definition of statutory rape and learning to act like an adult if she wanted to be treated like one, had not made a memorable impact. "I'm going to have to ground her. That's all there is to it."

But dealing with her sister's rash choices didn't get Tio Papi to the doctor's office. Gina slipped her fingers beneath the base of her wavy brunette ponytail to massage the tension gathering at the nape of her neck.

Derek nudged her with his elbow. "Need a ride home tonight?"

Missing the point! Although, in his defense, Derek was only hearing half the conversation. Gina summoned a smile for the friend she'd been riding a squad car with for almost two years now. "It's okay. Just a miscommunication at home."

"Gotta love our families, right?" Derek teased. She knew he had a strained relationship with his father. And there was no love lost for Derek's mother, who'd divorced his father and moved away, leaving her teenage son behind to be raised by an aging hippie who had trouble keeping a job and staying out of jail.

A difficult upbringing was part of the common ground they shared, and had helped solidify their working relationship and understanding of each other. Gina gave the sarcasm right back, whispering so her great-aunt couldn't hear. "Do we really have to?"

Derek grinned and directed her back to her phone. "Tell Aunt Lupe hi for me, okay?"

"I will. Tia Mami, Derek says hi."

"You teach that young man to say *hola*, and bring him to dinner sometime."

"I'm working on it." Gina continued the conversation with appropriate responses while her great-aunt rattled on about other concerns she'd have to deal with once she got home. While Lupe talked, Gina concentrated on the scenery as they drove past, partly because it was her job to observe the neighborhood and take note of anything that looked suspicious or unsafe, and partly because she'd already heard the same worried speech too many times before about fast cars and traffic accidents, young men who didn't come to the door to pick up a date and Uncle Rollo's deteriorating health.

Now *there* was something different. Gina lifted her chin for a better look. A tall man in silver and black running gear came around the corner off Pennsylvania Avenue and ran down the narrow side street. A jogger in this neighborhood was unusual. Maybe he was one of those yuppie business owners who'd opened an office in this part of town for a song, or he'd bought a loft in one of the area's abandoned warehouses, thinking he could revitalize a little part of Kansas City. Not for the first time, she considered the irony of people with money moving into this part of the city, while the natives like her were doing all they could to raise enough money to move out.

But irony quickly gave way to other thoughts. The runner was tall, lean and muscular. Although the stocking cap and wraparound sunglasses he wore masked the top half of his head, the well-trimmed scruff of brown beard on his golden skin was like catnip to her. Plus, she could tell he was fit by the rhythmic clouds of his breath in the cold air. He wasn't struggling to maintain that pace and, for a woman who worked hard to stay physically fit, she appreciated his athleticism.

As they passed each other, he offered her a polite wave, and Gina nodded in return. Since he already knew she'd been staring, she shifted her gaze to the side mirror to watch him run another block. Long legs and a tight butt. Gina's lips curved into a smile. They probably had a lot of scenery like that in the suburbs. A relationship was one thing she didn't have time for at this point in her life. And no way did she want to tie herself to anyone from the neighborhood who might want her to stay. But there was no harm in looking and getting her blood circulating a little faster. After all, it was only twenty-two degrees out, and a woman had to do whatever was necessary to stay warm.

Gina glanced over at her partner. Derek was handsome in his own way. He, too, had brown hair, but his smooth baby face was doing nary a thing for her circulation.

"Do we need to take a detour to your house and have a conversation with your sister? I'd be happy to um, have a word, with that boyfriend of hers." He took his hands off the steering wheel to make air quotes around *have a word*, as if he had ideas about roughing up Bobby on her behalf. As if she couldn't take care of her family's issues herself.

Since the car was moving, Gina guided one hand back to the steering wheel and changed the subject. She covered the speaker on her phone and whispered, "Hey, since things are quiet right now, why don't you swing by a coffee shop and get us something hot to drink. I haven't been able to shake this chill since that first snow back in October."

Although the remembered impression of Sexy Jogger Guy made that last sentence a lie, her request had the desired effect of diverting Derek's interest in her family problems.

"That I can do. One skinny mocha latte coming up."

Distracted with his new mission, Derek turned the squad car onto a cross street, plowing through a dip filled with dirty slush as they continued their daily patrol through the aging neighborhood. With houses and duplexes so close together that a person could barely walk between them, vehicles parked bumper-to-bumper against the curb and junk piling on porches and spilling into yards, this was a part of the city she knew far too well. Add in the branches of tall, denuded maple trees heavy with three months' worth of snow arching over the yards and narrow streets, and Gina felt claustrophobic. As much as she loved Kansas City and her job as a police officer, she secretly wondered if she was the reincarnation of some Central American ancestor and was meant for living on the high, arid plains of her people with plenty of blue sky and wide-open space, without a single snowflake in sight.

Setting aside her own restless need to escape, Gina turned toward the passenger door to find some privacy for this personal conversation. "Did you call Sylvie?" she asked her great-aunt, once the older woman's need to vent had subsided.

"She don't answer."

"What about Javi?" Her brother, Javier, was twenty-one, although that didn't necessarily mean he was making better choices than Sylvie. She kept hoping for the day when he would step up as the man of the family and allow their great-uncle to truly enjoy his retirement. "Can he drive you?"

"He's already gone. He's picking up some extra hours at work."

Well, that was one plus in the ongoing drama that was Gina's life. Maybe so long as Javi was intent on saving up to buy a truck, he would focus on this job and avoid the influence of his former friends who'd made some less productive choices with their lives, like stealing cars, selling drugs and running with gangs. "Good."

"Papi says he can drive," Lupe Molina offered in a hushed, uncertain tone.

Gina sat up as straight as her seat belt and protective vest allowed. "No. Absolutely not. The whole reason he's going for these checkups is because he passed out the last time his blood pressure spiked. He can't be behind the wheel."

"What do I do?" Lupe asked quietly.

As much as she loved her great-aunt and -uncle who'd taken in the three Galvan siblings and raised them after their mother had died, Lupe and Rollo Molina were now both close to eighty and didn't need the hassle of dealing with an attention-craving teenager. Especially not with

Rollo's health issues. "I'll call Sylvie. See if I can get her home to help like she promised. If you don't hear from her or me in ten minutes, call the doctor's office and reschedule the appointment for tomorrow. I'll be off except for practicing for my next SWAT test on the shooting range. I'll make sure you get there."

"All right. I can do that. You see? This is where having a young man to help you would be a good thing."

Gina rolled her eyes at the not-so-subtle hint. There was more than one path to success besides getting married and making babies. "I love you, Tia Mami. *Adios*."

"*Te amo*, Gina. You're always my good girl."

By the time she disconnected the call, Derek had pulled the black-and-white into the coffee shop's tiny parking lot but was making no effort to get out and let her deal with her family on her own. Instead, he rested the long black sleeve of his uniform on the steering wheel and grinned at her. "Sylvie off on another one of her escapades?"

Gina might as well fill in the blanks for him. "She's supposed to be driving my uncle to the doctor. Instead, she's cruising around the city with a young man who's too old for her."

Derek shook his head. "She does look older than seventeen when she puts on all her makeup." He dropped his green-eyed gaze to her black laced-up work boots. "She's got the family legs, too."

Ignoring the gibe at her five-foot-three-inch height, Gina punched in Sylvie's number. Then she punched Derek's shoulder, giving back the teasing camaraderie they shared. "You're eye-balling my little sister?"

"Hey, when you decorate the Christmas tree, you're supposed to celebrate it."

"Well, you don't get to hang any ornaments on my sister, understand? She's seventeen. You could get into all kinds of trouble with the department. And me."

Derek raised his hands in surrender. "Forget the department. You're the one who scares me. You're about to become one of SWAT's finest. I'm not messing with anyone in your family."

The call went straight to Sylvie's voice mail. "Damn it." Gina tucked her phone back into her vest and held her hand out for Derek's. "Could I borrow yours? Maybe if she doesn't recognize the number, she'll pick up."

"That means I'll have her number in my phone, you know. And Sylvie *is* a hottie."

"Seven. Teen." Gina repeated the warning with a smile and typed in her wayward sister's number.

She'd barely been a teenager herself when her mother had passed away and their long-absent father had willingly signed away his parental rights, leaving the three Galvans orphans in No-Man's Land, one of the toughest neighborhoods in downtown Kansas City. They'd moved out of their cramped apartment into a slightly less cramped house. Instead of prostitutes, drug dealers and gangbangers doing business beneath Gina's bedroom window, they'd graduated to the vicinity of a meth lab, which KCPD had eventually closed down, at the end of the block. Naturalized citizens who were proud to call themselves Americans, her great-aunt and -uncle had stressed the values of education and hard work, and they'd grown up proud but poor. With her diminutive stature, Gina had quickly learned how to handle herself in a fight and project an attitude so that no one would mess with her family or take advantage of her. That hardwired drive to protect her loved ones had morphed into a desire to protect any innocent who needed her help, including this neighborhood and her entire city. But she couldn't forget which side of the tracks the Galvans and Molinas had come from—and just how far she had to go to secure something better for them.

"Hey, don't jinx the SWAT thing for me, okay?" A little bit of her great-aunt and -uncle's superstitious nature buzzed through her thoughts like an annoying gnat she thought she'd gotten rid of. If she made Special Weapons and Tactics, the rise in status with the department and subsequent raise in pay would finally allow her to move her whole family into a house with a real yard in a safer suburb. She wasn't afraid of setting goals and working hard to achieve them, but it was rare that she allowed anything so personal as wanting some open space to plant a proper garden or get a dog or owning a bathroom she didn't have to share with four other people to motivate her. "I'm not the only recruit on Captain Cutler's list of candidates for the new SWAT team he's forming. There are ten people on a list for five spots. Including you."

"Yeah, but you're the toughest."

"Jinxing, remember?" Gina crossed her fingers and kissed her knuckles before touching them to her heart, a throwback from her childhood to cootie shots and negating bad karma. "We all have our talents."

"I'm just repeating what Cutler said at the last training meeting. McBride scored the highest at the shooting range. And you, my kickass little partner, are the one he said he'd least like to face one-on-one in a fight. Take the compliment."

It was on the tip of her tongue to remind Derek that she wasn't his *little* anything, but she was dealing with enough conflict already today. "You're doing well, too, or you'd have been eliminated already. Captain Cutler announces things like that so we stay competitive."

"Hey, I'm not quittin' anything until those new

promotions are posted. I only have to be fifth best and I'll still make the team."

"Fifth best?" Gina laughed. "Way to aim high, Johnson."

"It's too bad about Cho, though. He's been acing all the written tests and procedure evaluations."

Gina agreed. Colin Cho was a fellow SWAT candidate who'd suffered three cracked ribs when he'd been shot twice while directing traffic around a stalled car on the North Broadway Freeway in the middle of the night two weeks ago. Only his body armor had prevented the incident from becoming a fatality. "Any idea how he's doing?"

"I heard he's up and around, but he won't be running any races soon. He's restricted to desk duty for the time being. I wonder if they'll replace him on the candidate list or just shorten it to nine potential SWAT officers."

"Cho's too good an officer to remove from contention," Gina reasoned, hitting the phone icon on the screen to connect the call.

"But there *is* a deadline," Derek reminded her. "If he can't pass the physical…"

The number rang several times before her sister finally picked up. "Sylvie Galvan's phone," a man answered.

Not her sister but that slimy lothario who struck Gina as a mobster wannabe—if he wasn't already running errands and doing small jobs for some of the bigger criminals in town. Gina swallowed the curse on her tongue. She needed to keep this civil if she wanted to get her great-aunt and -uncle the help they needed. "Bobby, put Sylvie on."

"It's your wicked big sister," he announced. The sounds of horns honking and traffic moving in the background told her they were in his car. Hopefully, in the front seat and not stretched out together in the back. "What will you give me to hand you this phone?"

That teasing request was for her sister.

Gina cringed at the high-pitched sound of her sister's giggles. She groaned at the wet, smacking sound of a kiss. Or two. So much for keeping it civil. "Bobby Estes, you keep your hands off my sister or I will—"

"Blah, blah, blah." Sylvie was on the line now. Finally. She could live without the breathless gasps and giggles and the picture the noises created of a practically grown man making out with her innocent sister. "What do you want?"

"You forgot Tio Papi's doctor's appointment." Better to stick to the purpose of the phone call than to get into another lecture about the bad choices Sylvie was making. "You promised me you would drive him today."

"Javi can do it."

"He's at work. Besides, it was your responsibility." Her fingers curled into a fist at the sound of her sister's gasp. Really? Bobby couldn't keep his hands to himself for the ten seconds it would take to finish this call? "Do you want me to treat you like a grown-up or not?"

"I just got home from school."

"A half hour ago. I was counting on you. This isn't about me. It's about helping Rollo and Lupe. Do you want to explain to them why you've forgotten them?"

Bobby purred against her sister's mouth, and the offensive noise crawled over Gina's skin. "Is big sis being a downer again? You know she's jealous of us. Hang up, baby."

"Bobby, stop." Sylvie sounded a little irritated with her boyfriend. For once. The shuffling noises and protests made her think Sylvie was pushing him away. Gina suppressed a cheer. "When is the appointment?"

"Four forty-five. Can you do it?"

"Yeah. I can help." Thank goodness Sylvie still had enough little girl in her to idolize her pseudo grandparents. She'd do for them what she wouldn't do for Gina. Or herself, unfortunately. Her tone shifted to Bobby. "I need to go home."

"I said I was taking you out to dinner. I was gonna show you my friend's club," he whined. "Just because Gina's a cop, she doesn't make the rules. She sure as hell isn't in charge of what I do."

"Don't get mad, Bobby. Just drive me home."

Sylvie was doing some purring of her own. "I'll make it up to you later."

"Promise?"

"Promise."

"Ooh, I like it when you do that, baby."

Gina wished she could reach through the phone and yank her sister out of Bobby's car before she got into the kind of trouble that even a big sister with a badge couldn't help her with. "Sylvie?"

"I'll call Tia Mami and tell her we're on our way."

"Bobby doesn't need to go with you." A powerful car engine revved in the background. "Seeing him will only upset—"

"Bye."

Bobby shouted an unwanted goodbye. "Bye-bye, big sis."

She groaned when her sister's phone went silent. Gina cursed. "Have I ever mentioned how much I want to use Bobby Estes as one of the dummies in our fight-training classes?"

Derek laughed as he put away his phone. "Once or twice." He opened his door, and Gina shivered at the blast of wintry wind. "I keep telling you that I'd be happy to help run him in."

At least the chill helped some of her temper dissipate, as did Derek's unflinching support. "Bobby's too squeaky clean for that. He does just enough to annoy me, but not enough that I can prove he's committing any kind of crime. And Sylvie isn't about to rat him out."

"Just say the word, and I'm there for you, G." He turned to climb out. "I'll leave the car running so you stay warm."

But the dispatch radio beeped, and he settled back behind the wheel to listen to the details of the all-call. "So much for coffee."

Derek closed the door as the dispatch repeated. "Attention all units in the Westport area. We have a 10-52 reported. Repeat, domestic dispute report. Approach with caution. Suspect believed to be armed with a knife."

"That's the Bismarck place." Derek frowned as he shifted the cruiser into Drive and pulled out onto the street. "I thought Vicki Bismarck took out a restraining order against her ex."

"She did." This wasn't the first time they'd answered a call at the Bismarcks' home. The address was just a couple of blocks from their location. Gina picked up the radio while Derek flipped on the siren and raced through the beginnings of rush-hour traffic. "Unit 4-13 responding."

Her family troubles were forgotten as she pulled up the suspect's name on the laptop mounted on the dashboard. Domestic-disturbance calls were her least favorite kind of call. The situations were unpredictable, and there were usually innocent parties involved. This one was no different.

"Gordon Bismarck. I don't think he's handling the divorce very well." Gina let out a low whistle. "He's got so many D&Ds and domestic-violence calls the list goes on to a second page. No outstanding warrants, though, so we can't just run him in." She glanced over at Derek as they careened around a corner. "Looks like he's not afraid to hurt somebody. You ready for this?"

"I know you've got my back. And I've got yours."

She hoped he meant it because when they pulled up in front of the Bismarck house, they weren't alone. And the men belonging to a trio of motorcycles and a beat-up van didn't look like curiosity seekers who'd gathered to see what all the shouting coming from inside the bungalow was about.

Derek turned off the engine and swore. "How many thugs does it take to terrorize one woman? I hope Vicki's okay. Should I call for reinforcements?"

"Not yet." Gina tracked the men as they put out cigarettes and split up to block the end of the driveway and the sidewalk leading to the front door. Middle-aged. A couple with potbellies. One had prison tats on his neck. Another took a leisurely drink from a flask before tucking it inside the sheepskin-lined jacket he wore.

Their bikes were in better shape than they were. But any one of them could be armed. And she could guess that the guy with the flask wasn't the only one who'd been drinking. Judging by what she'd read on the cruiser's computer screen, these were friends, if not former cell mates, of Gordon Bismarck's. Gina's blood boiled in her veins at the lopsided odds. She reached for the door handle. "But keep your radio at the ready."

Gina pushed open the cruiser door and climbed out. "Gentlemen." She rested her hand on the butt of her holstered Glock. "I need you to disperse."

"You *need* us, *querida*?" Flask Man's leer and air kisses weren't even close to intimidating, and she certainly wasn't his *darling* anything.

Derek circled the cruiser, positioning himself closer to the two in the driveway while she faced off against the two on the sidewalk. "In case you don't understand the big word, you need to get on your bikes and ride away."

"We gave Gordy a ride home," Potbelly #1 said, thumbing over his shoulder just as something made of glass shattered inside the house.

A woman's voice cried out, "Gordon, stop it!"

"I paid for this damn house. And I'll—"

Gina needed to get inside to help Vicki Bismarck. But she wasn't going to leave these four aging gangbangers out here where they could surround the house or lie in wait for her and Derek to come back outside. "We're not interested in you boys today," she articulated in a sharp, authoritative tone. "But if you make me check the registrations on your bikes or van, or I get close enough to think any of you need a Breathalyzer test, then it *will* be about you."

Prison Tat Guy was the first to head toward his bike. "Hey, I can't have my parole officer gettin' wind of this."

Potbelly #2 quickly followed suit. "I'm out of here, man. Gordy doesn't need us to handle Vic. My old lady's already ticked that I stayed out all night."

Potbelly #1 clomped the snow off his boots before climbing inside the van. But he sat with the door open, looking toward the man with the flask. "What do you want me to do, Denny? I told Gordy I'd give him a ride back to his place."

Flask Man's watery brown eyes never left Gina's. "We ain't doin' nothing illegal here, *querida*. We're just a bunch of pals hangin' out at a friend's place."

"It's *Officer Galvan* to you." She had to bite down on the urge to tell him in two languages exactly what kind of man he was. But she wasn't about to give this patronizing lowlife the satisfaction of losing her temper. She was a cop. Proud of it. And this guy was about to get a lesson in understanding exactly who was in charge here. "Mr. Bismarck isn't going to need a ride." Potbelly #1 slammed his door and started the van's engine. Gina smiled at Flask Man and pulled out her handcuffs. "Denny, is it? I've got plenty of room in the backseat for both you and good ol' Gordy." She moved toward him, dangling the cuffs in a taunt to emphasize her words. "How do impeding an officer in the performance of her duty, aiding and abetting a known criminal, public intoxication and operating a vehicle under the influence sound to you?"

"You can't arrest me for all that."

"I wouldn't test that theory if I were you." Derek stepped out of the way of the van as it backed out of the driveway and sped after the two men on motorcycles. "Not with her."

Gina was close enough to see Flask Man's nostrils flaring with rage. "Handcuffs or goodbye?"

"I don't like a woman telling me what to do," he muttered, striding toward his bike. "Especially one like you." Once he was astraddle, he revved the engine, yelling something at Derek that sounded a lot like a warning to keep his woman in check. The roar of the bike's motor drowned out his last parting threat as he raced down the street, but Gina was pretty sure it had something to do with her parentage and how their next meeting would have a very different ending.

"Make sure they stay gone," Gina said, hooking her cuffs back onto her belt and running to the front door. She opened the glass storm door and knocked against the inside door. "KCPD!" she announced. The woman screamed, and the man yelled all kinds of vile curses. "Vicki Bismarck, are you all right? This is the police, answering a call to this address. I'm coming inside."

Twenty minutes later, Gina and Derek had Gordon Bismarck and his former wife, Vicki, separated into two rooms of their tiny, trashed home. Gina had bagged the box cutter Gordon had dropped when she'd pulled her gun and blinked her watery eyes at the stench of alcohol, vomit and sweat coming off Gordon's body. Either Gordy and his buddies had been beefing up their courage for this confrontation or they'd partied hard and gotten stupid enough to think violating a restraining order was a good idea.

Although the slurred epithets were still flying from the living room where Derek had taken Gordon to put a winter coat on over his undershirt, and Vicki was bawling in the kitchen while Gina tried to assess the woman's injuries, Gina was already wrapping up this case in her head. Even if Vicki refused to press charges, she could book Gordon on breaking and entering, violating his restraining order and public intoxication—all of which should keep him out of Vicki's life long enough for her to get the help she needed.

If she'd ask for it. Clearly, this wasn't the Bismarcks' first rodeo with KCPD. That probably explained why Gordon had brought his friends.

Although she hadn't noted any stab wounds on Vicki, the woman was cradling her left arm as if it had been yanked or twisted hard enough to do some internal damage. Gina glanced around at the slashed curtains and overturned chairs in the kitchen, her gaze landing on the shattered cell phone in the corner that had been crushed beneath a boot or hurled across the room. Clearly, there'd been a substantial altercation here.

Gina righted one of the chairs and urged the skinny woman to sit. "Will you let me look at that arm?" Gina asked, tearing off a fresh paper towel for the woman to dab at her tears. When Vicki nodded, Gina knelt beside her. Bruise marks that fit the span of a man's hand were already turning purple around her elbow. But there didn't seem to be any apparent deformity suggesting a broken bone. Didn't mean it hadn't been twisted savagely, spraining muscles and tendons. Gina pushed to her feet and headed toward the refrigerator-freezer. "An ice pack should help with the swelling."

She heard a crash from the living room and spun around as Derek cursed. "Gina—heads up!"

"Are you turnin' me in, you bitch? My boys are gonna kill you!"

"Gordy!" Vicki screamed as Gordon charged into the kitchen.

Chapter Two

Gina simply reacted, putting herself between the frightened woman and the red-faced man. There was no time to wonder how the drunk had gotten away from Derek. She ducked beneath the attacker's fist, kicked out with her leg, tripped the big brute, then caught his arm and twisted it behind his back, following him down to the floor. Before his chin smacked the linoleum, she had her knee in his back, pinning him in place.

"He's too big for the damn cuffs," Derek shouted, running in behind the perp. He knelt on the opposite side, catching the loose chain that was only connected to one wrist.

Gordon Bismarck writhed beneath her, trying to wrestle himself free. His curses switched from Vicki to Gina to women in general. Locking her own handcuffs around his free arm, Gina twisted his wrist and arm another notch until he yelped. "Don't make me mad, Mr. Bismarck. Your buddies outside already put me in a mood."

The mention of his friends sparked a new protest. "Denny! Al! Jim! I need—"

"Uh-uh." She pushed his cheek back to the floor. "They went bye-bye. Now you be a good boy while my partner walks you out to the squad car so you can sober up and chill that temper."

"My boys left?"

"That's right, Gordy." Derek wiped a dribble of blood from beneath his nose while Gina locked the ends of both cuffs together, securing him. "You're on your own."

"I don't want him touchin' me," Gordy protested. "I don't want him in my house."

"Not your choice." Gina stayed on top of the captive, her muscles straining to subdue him until he gave up the fight. She glanced up at Derek, assessing his injury. Other than the carpet lint clinging to his dark uniform from a tussle of some kind, he wasn't seriously hurt. Still, she kept her voice calm and firm, trying to reassure Vicki that they could keep her safe. "You got him okay?"

"I got him. Thanks for the save. I didn't realize the cuff wasn't completely closed around his fat wrist, and I ended up with an elbow in my face." Derek pulled the man to his feet, his bruised ego making him a little rough as he shoved Bismarck toward the front door. "Forget the coat. Now we can add assaulting a police officer to your charges. Come on, you lousy son of a…"

The door banged shut as Derek muscled Bismarck outside. Gina inhaled several deep breaths, cooling her own adrenaline rush. She watched from the foyer until she saw her partner open the cruiser and unceremoniously dump the perp into the backseat. Only after Derek had closed the door and turned to lean his hip against the fender did she breathe a sigh of relief. The situation was finally secure.

When he pulled out a cigarette and started to light it, Gina muttered a curse beneath her breath. She immediately thumbed the radio clipped to the shoulder of her uniform. "Derek," she chided, wanting to warn him it was too soon to let down his guard. "Call the sit-rep in to Dispatch, and tell them we'll be bringing in the suspect. I'll finish getting the victim's statement."

"Chill, G. Let a man catch his breath." He lit the cigarette and exhaled a puff before answering. "Roger that."

Gina shook her head. She supposed that losing control of the perp had not only dinged his ego but also rattled him. Maybe she should have a low-key chat with her partner. Aiming for fifth place wasn't going to get the job done. If he didn't light a fire under his butt and start showing all the ways he could excel at being a cop, Captain Cutler might cut him from the SWAT candidate list altogether.

But she had more pressing responsibilities to

attend to right now than to play the bossy big sister role with her partner and nudge Derek toward success. After softly closing the front door on the cold and the visual of Gordon Bismarck spewing vitriol in the backseat of the cruiser while Derek smacked the window and warned him to be quiet, Gina pulled out her phone again and returned to the kitchen. She found Vicki making a token effort to clean up some of the mess.

"Is he gone?" the woman asked in a tired voice. Although the tears had stopped, her eyes were an unnaturally bright shade of green from all her crying.

"He's locked in the back of the police cruiser, and I sent his friends away. He won't get to you again. Not today. Not while I'm here."

"Thank you." Vicki dropped a broken plate into the trash. "And Derek's okay?"

"'Derek'?"

"Officer Johnson." A blush tinted Vicki's pale cheeks. "I thought maybe Gordy thought…having another man in the house…" She shrugged off the rambling explanation. "I remember you two from the last time you were here. So does Gordy."

"I'm sure Officer Johnson will be fine. May I?" Gina held up her phone and, at Vicki's nod, snapped a couple of photos of the woman's injuries and sent them to her computer at work. "I'll need them to file my report."

"What if I refuse to press charges?" Vicki asked. "Gordy's friends might come back, even if he's not here. Denny's his big brother. He looks out for him."

Reminding herself that she hadn't lived Vicki Bismarck's life, and that the other woman probably had had the skills and confidence to cope with a situation like this beaten and terrorized out of her by now, Gina took a towel and filled it with some ice from the freezer. "I still have to take Mr. Bismarck in because he resisted arrest and assaulted an officer. And he's clearly violated his restraining order." She pressed the ice pack to Vicki's elbow and nodded toward the abrasion on her cheek. "You should get those injuries checked out by a doctor. Would you like me to call an ambulance?"

Vicki shook her head. "I can't afford that."

"How about I call another officer to take you to the ER? Or I can come back once we get your husband processed."

"No. No more cops, please." Vicki sank into a chair and rested her elbow on the table. "It just makes Gordy mad."

"What set him off this time?" Not that it mattered. Violence like this was never acceptable. But if Gina could get the victim talking, she might get some useful information to help get the repeat offender off the street and out of his wife's life. "I could smell the alcohol on him."

"He's been sleeping at Denny's house." Gina pulled out her notepad and jotted the name and information. "Gordy's been out of work for a while. Got laid off at the fertilizer plant. And I haven't been working long enough to get paid yet. I asked him if he'd picked up his unemployment check. He said he'd help me with groceries."

"And that set him off?"

"He doesn't like to talk about money. But no, as soon as I opened the door, he started yelling at me. Denny had said he saw me talking to another man." Vicki shrugged, then winced at the movement. "I just started a job at the convenience store a couple blocks from here. Guys come in, you know. I have to talk to them when I ring them up. I guess Denny told Gordy I was flirting."

Gina bit back her opinion of Gordy's obsession and maintained a cool facade. "When was the last time you ate?" If the woman needed money for groceries, Gina guessed it had been a while. She unzipped another pocket in her vest and pulled out an energy bar, pushing it into the woman's hand. "Here." She pulled out a business card for the local women's shelter as well, and handed it to Vicky. "You get hungry again, you go here, not to Gordy. They'll help you get groceries at the food pantry. Mention my name and they'll even sneak you an extra chocolate bar."

Finally, that coaxed a smile from the frightened woman. "I haven't eaten real chocolate in months. Sounds heavenly."

After getting a few more details about Vicki's relationship with Gordon and her injuries, Gina wrapped up the interview. "You need to be checked out by a doctor," she reiterated. "Sooner rather than later. Do you have a friend who can take you to the hospital or your regular doctor?"

"I can call my sister. She keeps nagging me to move in with her and her husband."

"Good." Gina handed Vicki her phone. "Why don't you go ahead and do that while I'm here?"

Vicki hesitated. "Will Gordy be back when I get home?"

"I can keep him locked up for up to forty-eight hours—longer if he doesn't make bail." Gina had a feeling Vicki's husband would be locked up for considerably longer than that but didn't want to guarantee anything she couldn't back up. "We can send a car through the neighborhood periodically to watch if his brother and friends come back. See a doctor. Go to your sister's, and get a good night's sleep. Call the shelter, and get the help you need."

"Thank you." Vicki punched in her sister's phone number and smiled again. "That was sweet to see you take Gordy down—and you aren't any bigger than I am. Maybe I should learn some of those moves."

Gina smiled back and pulled out her own business card. "It's all about attitude. Here. Call me when you're feeling up to it. A few other officers and I teach free self-defense training sessions."

Although Vicki didn't look entirely convinced that she could learn to stand up for herself, at least she had made arrangements with her sister and brother-in-law to stay with them for a few nights by the time Gina was closing the front door behind her and heading down the front walk toward the street. What passed for sunshine on the wintry day was fading behind the evening clouds that rolled across the sky and promised another dusting of snow. Despite the layers of the sweater, flak vest and long-sleeved uniform she wore, Gina shivered at the prospect of spring feeling so far out of reach.

Ignoring the glare of blurry-eyed contempt aimed at her from the backseat of the cruiser, Gina arched a questioning eyebrow at Derek. "Bismarck didn't hurt you, did he?"

Derek massaged the bridge of his nose that was already bruising and circled around the car as she approached. "Just my pride. I don't even know if the guy meant to clock me. But I was on the floor, and he was on his way to the kitchen before my eyes stopped watering."

"Ouch."

"Just don't tell anybody that a drunk got the

upper hand on me and you had to save my ass. I don't imagine that would impress Captain Cutler."

"We're a team, Derek. We help each other out."

"And keep each other's secrets?"

"Something like that."

His laughter obscured his face with a cloud of warm breath in the chilly air. "Now I really owe you that cup of coffee." Her aversion to the cold weather was hardly a secret compared to his possible incompetence in handling the suspect. Maybe her partner wasn't ready for the demands of the promotion. He pulled open his door. "Come on. Let's get you warmed up—"

The sharp crack of gunfire exploded in the cold air.

Derek's green eyes widened with shock for a split second before he crumpled to the pavement. "Derek!"

A second bullet thwacked against the shatterproof glass of the windshield. A third whizzed past her ear and shattered the glass in Vicki Bismarck's storm door. Gina pulled the Glock at her hip and dove the last few feet toward the relative shelter of the car. A stinging shot of lead or shrapnel burned through her calf, and she stumbled into the snow beside the curb.

Where were the damn shots coming from? Who was shooting? Had Denny Bismarck come back? She hadn't heard a motorcycle on the street. But then, he hadn't been alone, either.

"Derek? I need you to talk to me." There was still no answer. Bullets hit the cruiser and a tree trunk in the front yard. Several more shots scuffed through the snow with such rapidity that she knew the shooter either had an automatic weapon or several weapons that he could drop and keep firing. Gina crouched beside the wheel well, listening for the source of the ambush, praying there were no innocent bystanders in the line of fire. The bullets were coming from across the street. But from a house? An alley? A car?

"Derek?" The amount of blood seeping down her leg into her shoe told her the shooter was using something large caliber, meant to inflict maximum damage. But her wound was just a graze. She could still do her job. Before she sidled around the car to pull her partner to safety, Gina got on her radio and called it in. "This is Officer Galvan. Unit 4-13. Officers need assistance. Shots fired." She gave the street address and approximation of where she thought the shooter might be before repeating the urgent request, "Officers need assistance."

Gina stilled her breath and heard Gordon Bismarck cussing up a blue streak inside the cruiser. She'd heard Vicki screaming inside the house. What she didn't hear was her partner. Guilt and fear punched her in the stomach. She hadn't done job one and kept him safe. She hadn't had his back when he needed her most.

"Derek?" she called out one more time before cradling the gun in her hands. When she heard the unexpected pause between gunshots, she crept around the trunk of the car, aiming her weapon toward the vague target of the shooter. "Police! Throw down your weapon!" she warned.

A quick scan revealed empty house, empty alley, empty house…bingo! Driver in a rusty old SUV parked half a block down. Gina straightened. "Throw down your weapon, and get out of the vehicle!"

The man's face was obscured by the barrel of the rifle pointed at her.

There was no mistaking his intent.

Gina squeezed off a shot and dove for cover, but it was too late.

A bullet struck her in the arm, tearing through her right shoulder, piercing the narrow gap between her arm and her protective vest. She hit the ground, and her gun skittered from her grip. Unlike the graze along the back of her leg, she knew this wound was a bad one. The path of the bullet burned through her shoulder.

She clawed her fingers into the hardened layers of snow and crawled back into the yard, away from the shooter. It was hard to catch her breath, hard to orient herself in a sea of clouds and snow. She rolled onto her back, praying she wasn't imagining the sound of sirens in the distance, hating that she was certain of the grinding noise of the SUV's engine turning over.

She saw Vicki Bismarck hovering at her broken front door. When Gina turned her head the other direction, she looked beneath the car and saw Derek on the ground, unmoving. Was he even alive? "Derek?"

Did someone have a grudge against him? Against her? Against cops? She hadn't made any friends among Denny Bismarck and his crew. Was this payback for arresting his brother? For being bested by a woman?

Her shoulder ached, and her right arm was numb. Her chest felt like a boulder sat on it. Still, she managed to reach her radio with her other hand and tug it off her vest. The shooter's car was speeding away. She couldn't see much from her vantage point, couldn't read the license plate or confirm a make of vehicle. The leg wound stung like a hot poker through her calf, but the wound to her shoulder—the injury she could no longer feel—worried her even more. Finding that one spot beneath her armor was either one hell of a lucky shot or the work of a sharpshooter. Gina's vision blurred as a chill pervaded her body.

"Stay inside the house!" a man yelled. "Away from the windows."

She saw silver running pants and black shoes

stomping through the snow toward her. Gina tried to find her gun.

"Officer?" The tall jogger with the sexy beard scruff came into view as he knelt in the snow beside her. "It's okay, ma'am." His eyes were hidden behind reflective sunglasses, and he clutched a cell phone to his ear, allowing her few details as to what he looked like. He picked up her Glock from the snow where it had landed and showed it to her before tucking it into the back of his waistband. "Your weapon is secure."

She slapped her left hand against his knee and pulled at the insulated material there. "You have to stay down. Shooter—"

"He's driving away," the man said. She wasn't exactly following the conversation, but then he was talking on his cell phone as he leaned over her, running his free hand up and down her arms and legs. "No, I couldn't read the license. It was covered with mud and slush. Yes, just the driver. Look, I'll answer your questions later. Just get an ambulance here. Now!" He disconnected the call and stuffed the phone inside his pocket. He tossed aside his sunglasses and looked down into her eyes. Wow. He was just as good-looking up close as he'd been from a distance. "You hit twice?"

Gina nodded, thinking more about her observation than her answer. She reached up and touched her shaking fingertips to the sandpapery stubble that shadowed his jaw. "I know you." Before her jellified brain could place why he looked so familiar to her, he grabbed her keys off her belt and bolted to his feet. She turned her head to watch him unlock the trunk to get the med kit. How did he know it was stored there? He was acting like a cop—he'd provided the squad car number and street address on that phone call. He knew KCPD lingo and where her gear was stowed. "Captain Cutler?" That wasn't right. But the blue eyes and chiseled features were the same. But she'd never seen the SWAT captain with that scruffy catnip on his face.

She wasn't any closer to understanding what she was seeing when he knelt beside her again, opening the kit and pulling out a compress. She winced as he slipped the pad beneath her vest and pressed his hand against her wound to stanch the bleeding. The deep, sure tone of voice was a little like catnip to her groggy senses, too. "I'm Mike Cutler. I've had paramedic training. Lie still."

Why were her hormones involved in any of this conversation? She squeezed her eyes shut to concentrate. She was a KCPD police officer. She'd been shot. The perp had gotten away. There was protocol to follow. She had a job to do. Gina opened her eyes, gritting her teeth against the pressure on her chest and the fog inside her head. "Check my partner. He's hit."

"You're losing blood too fast. I'm not going anywhere until I slow the bleeding." The brief burst of clarity quickly waned. The Good Samaritan trying to save her life tugged on her vest the moment her eyes closed. "Officer Galvan? No, no, keep your eyes open. What's your first name?"

"Gina."

"Gina?" He was smiling when she blinked her eyes open. "That's better. Pretty brown eyes. Like a good cup of coffee. I want to keep seeing them, okay?" She nodded. His eyes were such a pretty color. No, not pretty. There wasn't anything *pretty* about the angles of his cheekbones and jaw. He certainly wasn't from this part of town. She'd have remembered a face like that. A face that was still talking. "Trust me. I'm on your side. If I look familiar, it's because you're a cop, and you probably know my dad."

Mike Cutler. My dad. Gina's foggy brain cleared with a moment of recognition. "Captain Cutler? Oh, God. I'm interviewing with him... Don't tell him I got shot, okay?" But he'd left her. Gina called out in a panic. "Cutler?"

"I'm here." Her instinct to exhale with relief ended up in a painful fit of coughing. "Easy. I was just checking your partner."

"How is he?"

"Unconscious. As far as I can tell, he has a gunshot wound to the arm. But he may have hit his head on the door frame or pavement. His nose is bruised."

"That was…before." She tried to point to the house.

"Before what?"

The words to explain the incident with Gordon Bismarck were lost in the fog of her thoughts. But her training was clear. Derek was shot. And she had a job to do.

"The prisoner?" Gina tried to roll over and push herself up, but she couldn't seem to get her arm beneath her. The snow and clouds and black running shoes all swirled together inside her head.

"Easy, Gina. I need you to lie still. An ambulance is on its way. You've injured your shoulder, and I don't see an exit wound. If that bullet is still inside you, I don't want it traveling anywhere." He unzipped his jacket and shrugged out of it. He draped the thin, insulated material over her body, gently but securely tucking her in, surrounding her with the residual warmth from his body and the faint, musky scent of his workout. "The guy in the backseat is loud, but unharmed. The lady at the front door looks scared, but she isn't shot. Lie down. You're going into shock." He pulled her radio from beneath the jacket and pressed the call button. "Get that bus to…" Gina's vision blurred as he rattled off the address. "Stay with me. Gina?" His warm hand cupped her face, and she realized just how cold she was. She wished she could wrap her whole body up in that kind of heat. She looked up into his stern expression. "Stay with me."

"Catnip."

"What?" Her eyelids drifted shut. "Gina!"

The last thing she saw was her blood seeping into the snow. The last thing she felt was the man's strong hands pressing against her breast and shoulder. The last thing she heard was his voice on her radio.

"Officer down! I repeat: officer down!"

Chapter Three

Six weeks later

"He shoots! He scores!" The basketball sailed through the hoop, hitting nothing but net. Troy Anthony spun his wheelchair on the polished wood of the physical therapy center's minicourt. His ebony braids flew around the mocha skin of his bare, muscular shoulders, and one fist was raised in a triumphant gloat before he pointed to Mike. "You are buying the beers."

"How do you figure that?" Mike Cutler caught the ball as it bounced past him, dribbled it once and shoved a chest pass at his smirking competitor. It was impossible not to grin as his best friend and business partner, Troy, schooled him in the twenty-minute pickup game. "I thought we were playing to cheer *me* up."

Troy easily caught the basketball and shoved it right back. "I was playing to win, my friend. Your head's not in the game."

Mike's hands stung, forgetting to catch the

pass with his fingertips instead of his palms. He *was* distracted. "Fine. Tonight at the Shamrock. Beers are on me."

He tucked the ball under his arm as he climbed out of the wheelchair he'd been using. Once his legs unkinked and the electric jolts of random nerves firing across his hips and lower back subsided, he pushed the chair across the polished wood floor to stow the basketball in the PT center's equipment locker. At least he didn't have to wear those joint pinching leg braces or a body cast anymore.

But he wasn't about to complain. Twelve years ago, he hadn't been able to walk at all, following a car accident that had shattered his legs from the pelvis on down, so he never griped about the damaged nerves or aches in his mended bones or stiff muscles that protested the changing weather and an early morning workout. As teenagers, Mike and Troy had bonded over wheelchair basketball and months of physical rehabilitation therapy with the woman who had eventually become Mike's stepmother. Unlike Mike, because of a gunshot wound he'd sustained in a neighborhood shooting, Troy would never regain the use of his legs. But the friendship had stuck, and now, at age twenty-eight, they'd both earned college degrees and had opened their own physical therapy center near downtown Kansas City.

"C'mon, man. Don't make me feel like I'm

beatin' up on ya. I said you didn't have to go back
to the chair to play me. I could beat you standing on your two feet. Today, at any rate." Troy
pushed his wheels once and coasted over to the
edge of the court beside Mike. His omnipresent
smile and smart-ass attitude had disappeared.
"Losing that funding really got to you, huh? Or
is this mood about a woman?"

He hadn't put his heart on the line and gotten
it stomped on by anyone of the female persua-
sion lately. Not since Caroline. "No. No woman."

Troy picked up a towel off the supply cart and
handed one to Mike, grinning as he wiped the
perspiration from his chest. "No woman? That
would sure put *me* in a mood."

"You're a funny guy, you know that," Mike
deadpanned, appreciating his friend's efforts to
improve his disposition. But he couldn't quite
shake the miasma of frustration that had plagued
his thoughts since opening that rejection letter in
the mail yesterday. "I had a brilliant idea, writing
that grant proposal." Mike toweled the dampness
from his skin before tossing Troy his gray uniform polo shirt. "We had enough money from
the bank loan and our own savings to get this
place built. But it's hardly going to sustain itself
with the handful of patients we have coming in.
If we were attached to a hospital—"

"We specifically decided against that." Troy
didn't have to remind him of their determination

to give back to the community. Mike opened the laundry compartment on the supply cart and Troy tossed both towels inside. "We wanted to be here in the city where the people who needed us most could have access to our services."

"I still believe in that." Mike stared at the CAPT logo for the Cutler-Anthony Physical Therapy Center embroidered on the chest of his own shirt before pulling it over his head and tugging the hem down to cover his long torso. "But those are the same people who don't always have insurance and can't always pay. I was certain that urban development grant for small businesses would help us."

"There'll be other grants." Troy donned his shirt and peeled off the fingerless gloves he wore when he played anything competitive in his wheelchair. "Caroline said she'd fund a grant for us. To thank you for being there when she needed you."

"And that would be right up until the night she turned down my proposal?" The fact that he could talk about it now told Mike that his ego had taken a bigger blow than his heart had. But that blow had been the third strike in the relationship game. He had no plans to step up to the plate and put his heart on the line anymore. If he couldn't tell the difference between a friends-with-benefits package and a connection that was leading to forever, he'd do well to steer clear of anything serious. He'd been the shoulder to cry on, the protective big brother and the best friend too many times to risk it. He could rely on his principles, his family and friends like Troy. But he wasn't about to rely on his heart again. "No. No asking Caroline. I didn't propose because I wanted her money, and I'm not going to take it now as a consolation prize."

Troy knew just how far he could push the relationship button before he made a joke. "Maybe you could hock the engagement ring. That'd keep us open another month."

Mike glared down at his friend for a moment before laughter shook through his chest. "More like a day and a half."

"Dude, no wonder she said no."

The shared laughter carried them through the rest of putting away the equipment they'd used and prepping for their first—and, as far as Mike knew, their only—appointment of the morning. But even Troy's mood had sobered by the time they headed toward the door leading into the entry area and hallway that led to a row of offices and locker rooms. "You're a smart guy, Mikey. You'll figure out a way to keep us solvent."

"Without losing your apartment or my house?"

"I'd be happy to go out and recruit us more female clientele. It's Ladies' Night at the Shamrock tonight. I can pour on some of that legendary Anthony charm."

"Creeper."

"You got a better plan?"

"Not at the moment."

"You're thinkin' too hard on this, Mike. We haven't even been open a year. We'll get more paying customers soon. I feel it in my bones." He held up a fist and waited for Mike to absorb some of his positive thinking.

Trusting his friend's outlook more than his own, Mike bumped his fist against Troy's. "I just have to be patient, right?"

"Nobody waits out trouble better than you."

Mike shook his head. "Is that supposed to be a compli—?" The door opened before they reached it, and the center's office manager, Frannie Mesner, stepped into the gym. "Good morning."

"Hey, Sun...shine." Troy's effusive greeting fell flat when they saw the puffy, red-rimmed eyes behind Frannie's glasses. He rolled his chair over to get a box of tissues off the supply cart and take them to her. She sniffed back a sob as she took the box.

Was she hurt? Had she gotten some bad news? Mike moved in beside her and dropped a comforting arm around her trembling shoulders. "Frannie?"

The flush of distress on Frannie's pale cheeks made her freckles disappear. She pulled out a handful of tissues and dabbed her eyes before blowing her nose. "Leo gets released on parole today."

Her ex. She wasn't hurt. But definitely bad news.

"Has he contacted you?" Mike asked.

"He's not supposed to."

"Has he contacted you?" he repeated, articulating the protective concern in his voice. Frannie shook her head, stirring short wisps of copper hair over her damp cheeks.

Troy set the tissue box in his lap. "Is the restraining order still in effect?"

Mike watched the confidence she'd built over the past few months disappear in the span of a few heartbeats.

When she didn't answer, Mike pulled away to face her. "Take a few minutes to call your attorney and make sure it is. If not, make an appointment to get it reinstated. Troy or I can go with you, if you want."

Troy slid Frannie a worried glance before spinning away from the conversation to return the box to its shelf. "Yeah. I can do that. We'd have to take my van, though. If you don't mind riding shotgun. And you trust my driving."

What happened to that legendary Anthony charm? The Troy he knew was all mouth and swagger 99 percent of the time. Except when it came to the office manager Mike had hired for their fledgling physical therapy center. Frannie had been their first client. But more than rebuilding her physical strength after a beatdown from her ex that had cost her the sight in one eye, she had needed a job, and Mike and Troy had provided it. He suspected she also appreciated the office's predictable routine and the haven of a well-built workplace run by the son of a cop and a paraplegic, whose friends were also cops.

Mike might not carry a gun but, because of his dad and friends at KCPD, he knew how to keep a woman safe. Avoiding dangerous situations in the first place was rule one. "You know we'll give you the time off for personal business like that. Make sure that protection order is in place. Beyond that, Troy or I will escort you to your car and follow you home. You notify the police if he calls or you see his face anywhere close to you."

"I can swing by your place and double check the locks on the windows and door," Troy offered.

Mike nodded. "Sounds like a plan."

"My building isn't handicapped accessible." Frannie sniffed away the last of her tears and dabbed at the pink tip of her nose. "I'm sorry."

Troy shrugged, then reached for her hand. There was definitely something going on with him where Frannie was concerned. "Don't you apologize for that."

Mike wasn't sure how to help his friend, other

than alleviate his concern about Frannie. "I'll stop by after work, then."

At least she felt safe here at the clinic. She tucked the used tissues into the pocket of her khaki slacks and dredged up a shy smile. "You guys are the best bosses ever. Thank you." Although she'd started the job with no secretarial experience, Frannie had eventually found her feet and her own system of organization that worked—for her. And, when she wasn't afraid for her life like she was this morning, she was a friendly, quiet presence who made their patients feel welcome at the clinic. She wound her arm around Mike's waist and squeezed him in a shy hug. "Thanks." She turned toward Troy with her arms outstretched and leaned over to give him a hug, too. "Thank you."

Troy turned his nose into her hair, breathing deeply. "No sweat, Sunshine."

Either sensing Troy's interest or feeling a similar longing herself, Frannie quickly pulled away and tipped her face to Mike. "Your eight o'clock appointment is here. He's already changing in the locker room."

Chaz Kelly, a retired firefighter with a new knee, opened the door behind Frannie, startling her. "Hey, pretty lady. You weren't at your desk to greet me this morning when I checked in." Bald and blustery, his gaze darted over to Troy and Mike. "Morning, boys. Ready to put this fat old man through his paces?"

Frannie's body visibly contracted away from Chaz's pat on her shoulder. Uh-huh. So much for feeling safe. She scooted closer to Troy's chair and didn't look any more comfortable there. "Your dad is here, too, Mike."

"Here?" It was rarely a good thing for the supervisor of KCPD's SWAT teams to make a surprise visit. Mike's concern instantly went to his stepmother and much younger half brother. "Is everything okay? Jillian? Will?"

"He didn't say. But I think it's work related. He's in uniform. There's someone with him. I put them in your office. I'll go start a pot of coffee." Her hand went self-consciously to one tear-stained cheek. "And wash my face."

As Frannie left, Mike pulled his phone from his pocket, wondering if he'd missed a text or call during the basketball game. The lack of messages altered his concern into curiosity.

Troy tapped his fist against Mike's arm and pointed at the door. "I got this. Better not keep the captain waiting." Troy spun his chair around toward the door on the far side of the half gym that led to the equipment room and treatment tables. "Come on, Chaz. Let's get you on the treadmill and get you warmed up. Did you stick to that diet we gave you?"

Their conversation faded as Mike hurried

down the outer hallway to his office. "Dad?" Michael Cutler Sr. was on his feet to greet him with a handshake and a hug when Mike rounded the corner into his office. "Hey. Everything okay?"

"Not to worry. I'm fine. The family's fine."

Both standing at six-four, father and son looked each other in the eye as Mike pulled away. "What's up?" His eyes widened when he saw the petite woman waiting behind his father. "Officer Galvan."

Her dark eyes shared his surprise. "Catnip…" Mike arched his brows at her stunned whisper. She blinked away the revelation of emotion. "It *was* you."

"Excuse me?"

Gina Galvan was shorter than he remembered. Of course, his perspective was a little different, standing upright versus kneeling over her supine body. Without the hazards of gunfire or a medical emergency to focus on, Mike stole a few seconds to take in details about his visitor. She'd changed her hair. Instead of a long ponytail spilling over the snow, short, loose waves danced against the smooth line of her jaw. She wore a black sling over her right shoulder, keeping her arm immobile against her stomach. And he shouldn't have noticed the athletic curves arcing beneath the narrow waist of her jeans. But he did.

"The day I got shot—you were the runner

who stopped to help us." Her gaze shifted between Mike and his father. "You two look so much alike, I guess I convinced myself I'd hallucinated you."

Mike chuckled at her admission. Although there was a peppering of gray in his dad's dark brown hair and Mike didn't shave as closely as KCPD regulations required, it wasn't the first time he'd been mistaken for his father. "I don't think I've ever been anyone's hallucination before. Fantasy, maybe, but…"

She frowned as if she didn't get the joke. His father looked away, embarrassed at his lame attempt at humor. Right. Leave the jokes to Troy.

The proud tilt of her chin and intense study from her dark eyes warned him that Gina Galvan wasn't inclined to laugh at much of anything. Which was a pity because he suddenly wondered what those pink lips would look like softened with a smile.

Reel it in, Cutler. Clearly, this wasn't a social call. And he already had enough on his plate without letting his errant hormones steer him into another misguided relationship.

Starched and pressed and always in charge of the room, Michael Sr. turned to include them both. "I wasn't sure you two would remember each other after a meeting like that. I guess there's no need for introductions."

"No, sir." Off-duty and out of uniform, she still talked like a cop.

"Nah." Mike invited them both to sit in the guest chairs in front of his desk before circling around to pull out his own chair. "How's the recovery going?" Gina's gaze drilled into his. He interpreted that as a *Don't ask.* "Did they catch the guy who did it?"

"No."

He'd suspected that was the case, or else a detective or investigator from the DA's office would have been back to question him on his account of the incident. "Sorry to hear that. And I'm sorry I couldn't give KCPD a better description of the shooter's SUV or license plate. The whole back end was covered in frozen mud and slush."

She nodded. "He probably went straight to a car wash afterward so we couldn't even look for a dirty vehicle."

"Probably. How's your partner?"

"Back on active duty."

"That's good news." Or not, judging by the scowl that darkened her expression. Even with a frown like that, Mike had a hard time calling Gina Galvan anything but pretty. High cheekbones. Full lips. Dark, sensuous eyes. Hair the color of dark-roast coffee. "You cut your hair since I saw you last."

"I was bleeding in the snow when you saw me

last." The subtle warmth of an accent made an intriguing contrast to the crisp snap of her words.

"I like it—the hair, not the blood. I didn't realize how wavy your hair was."

"Well, long hair is hardly practical with—" she gestured at her arm in the sling "—this. And I am not going to rely on my aunt or my sister to put my hair up every day."

"Sounds smart."

"Why are we talking about my hair?" The accent grew a little more pronounced as a hint of acid entered her tone. Was that anger? Frustration? A clear message that she wasn't interested in his compliments or flirtations—idle or otherwise. She froze for a moment before inhaling a deep breath. Then, oddly, she crossed her fingers and brushed them against her lips and heart before settling her hand back into her lap. He thought it must be some kind of calming ritual because her posture relaxed a fraction and the tension left her voice. "I owe you for saving my life, Mr. Cutler. Thank you."

He'd heard the gunshots on his morning run through the neighborhood just a mile or so from the clinic. What else was he supposed to do besides try to help? "It's just Mike. And you're welcome."

Was that what this visit was about? A proud woman wanting to thank him? But she'd indicated that she hadn't remembered him.

Mike's father clearly had a purpose for coming to the clinic. "Could you give us a few minutes, Galvan?"

Gina popped to her feet, eager to please the captain or simply eager to escape the uncomfortable conversation. "Yes, sir."

Mike stood, too, as Frannie stepped into the room carrying a tray of steaming coffee mugs with packets of sugar and creamer. He scooted aside a stack of bills for her to set the tray on his desk. "Thanks. Why don't you give Officer Galvan a tour of the facility while Dad and I talk."

"Okay." Frannie's eyes were still puffy behind her glasses, but the pale skin beneath her freckles and pixie haircut was back to normal. She smiled at Gina and led her into the hallway. "We can start with the women's locker room."

Mike closed the door and returned to his seat, looking across the desk as his father picked up a mug and blew the steam off the top. "How worried should I be about this impromptu visit?"

Chapter Four

His father pursed his lips and made a rare face before swallowing. "Um…"

Mike took a sip and spit the sour brew back into his mug. "Sorry about that. Frannie must have cleaned the coffeemaker out with vinegar again."

"Did she rinse it afterward?"

"I'll sneak in there and make a new pot later this morning while she's busy." Mike spun his chair and emptied his mug into the potted fern beside the door. "She's a little distracted. Her ex gets out on parole today."

"Leo Mesner?" Mike nodded, returning his mug to the tray. Michael Sr. followed his lead, dumping out his coffee. "I'll find out who Leo's parole officer will be so we can keep tabs on him for her."

"Thanks. After that last assault, he shouldn't have any contact with her, but you never know if prison sobered him up and made him rethink hurting his ex-wife or just made him even angrier and bent on revenge. We'll do what we can to keep her safe from this end, too."

"I know you will, son. You're too kindhearted for your own good."

"You know it's not all kindness, Dad." His father's blue eyes pierced right into Mike's soul, understanding his need to atone for the damage he'd done in his youth—and wishing his older son would forgive himself already. Mike smiled a reassurance to ease his father's concern. "But you didn't come here to talk about my problems. I'm assuming this visit has to do with Officer Galvan?"

His dad nodded. "I'm bringing you a new client."

He pointed briefly to his own shoulder. "She had surgery?"

"Stitches in her leg to seal up the bullet graze there. Emergency surgery to repair a nicked lung. She's recovered from those without incident." His dad's expression turned grim. "But the second bullet went through her shoulder and tore it up. The doctors had to rebuild the joint. The PT is for muscle and nerve damage there."

"What kind of nerve damage?"

"You're the expert. But I know it has affected her hand. She can't hold a gun."

"Only six weeks after getting shot? She shouldn't be trying."

"You don't know Gina." His dad leaned forward, sharing a confidence. "She's nobody's pretty princess. Not the easiest person to get along with, especially since the shooting. She's already quit one therapist, and another refused to work with her after the first session."

"But I'm so desperate for patients, you think I'll take her on?"

"No." He leaned back, his features carved with an astute paternal smile. "I know how tough you are. All you've survived and been through. I know how resourceful you can be. If anybody can stand up to Gina, it's you."

There was a compliment in there somewhere, one that ranked right up there with Troy's claim that he could outlast trouble. Maybe his dad and friend were subtly trying to tell him that he was too hardheaded for his own good. "What was the issue with the other therapists? She wouldn't do the work?"

"Just the opposite. She pushed herself too hard."

Mike nodded. "Did more damage than helped her recovery. You think Troy and I want to risk that kind of liability?"

"She's an ambitious woman. Trying to do better for herself and her family. Other than her great-uncle's disability and social security, she's their sole support. But she's a good cop. Good instincts. Well trained. Gina can think on her feet. Once the bad guys realize they've under-estimated her, they discover they don't want to mess with her. I was ready to put her on my new SWAT team until the shooting. I've still got a spot for her." His dad's shoulders lifted with a wry apology. "But if she can't handle the physical demands of the job, I can't use her."

"You want me to fix her so she can make the team?"

"I want you to fix her so we don't lose her to No-Man's Land." Just a few city blocks north of the clinic. Poverty, gangs, drugs, prostitution, homelessness—it was a tough place to grow up. His dad's second wife, Jillian, had barely sur-vived her time in one of Kansas City's most dan-gerous neighborhoods. Troy had almost lost his life there. Mike knew his father and his SWAT team had answered several calls there over the years. There was a lot to admire about a woman who held down a good job and took care of her family in the No-Man's Land neighborhood. In *this* neighborhood, where he and Troy were de-termined to make a difference. Michael Cutler Sr. was a professional hostage negotiator. He knew what buttons to push to ensure Mike's co-operation, and helping someone deserving in this part of the city was a big one. "Help her realize her potential. KCPD needs her. She needs the job, and I want her if she can do it."

Mike scrubbed his hand over the stubble shading his jaw before deciding to swallow a little pride. "Can she pay?"

"I'll cover whatever her department insurance doesn't."

"You believe in her that much?"

"I do."

"Then I will, too." Appreciating the faith his father had always had in him, Mike rolled his chair back and stood. "I'll get the job done for you, Dad."

"Thanks. I knew I could count on you." With their business completed, Michael Sr. stood as well, adjusting the gun at his hip and pulling the black SWAT cap from his back pocket. He tipped his head toward the unpaid bills that Mike had pushed aside earlier. "Did you get the grant?"

"No."

"I suppose applying to Caroline's foundation is out of the question."

"Yes."

He shook his head as he crossed to the door. "To be honest, I think you dodged a bullet there, son. Caroline was a nice girl. But Jillian and I were never so bored out of our minds that night we had dinner with her parents. And, of course, if she can't appreciate you for who you are and not who she wants you to be—"

"Yeah, yeah." Mike grinned, patting his dad's shoulder to stop that line of well-meaning conversation. "Nice Dad Speech."

"I'm really good at 'em, aren't I?" They shared a laugh until Michael Sr. paused with his hand on the door knob to ask, "Say, what was that 'cat-nip' thing about with Gina?"

"Beats me. She said it to me before she lost consciousness the day of the shooting. Maybe she was delirious and thinking about her pet."

They both suspected there was more to the story than that but Mike didn't have the answer. His dad paused before opening the door. "You'll give me regular reports on Gina's progress?"

"Does she know you're setting this up for her?"

"She knows I want her on my team and that I was happy to give her a ride this morning. She still can't drive for another two weeks."

"And she knows this is her last chance to get her recovery right in time for you to name the new SWAT team?"

"Very astute. You got your mother's brains." They stepped into the hallway and Michael Sr. pulled his SWAT cap on. "See you at Will's science fair presentation Thursday night?"

"I already told the squirt I'd be there."

A small parade, led by a grinning Troy, stopped them before they reached the clinic's entrance. Troy held out his hand. "Hey, Captain C. I wanted to make sure I said hi before you left."

"Troy." The two men exchanged a solid handshake. "Good to see you."

"You, too, sir."

Frannie and Gina waited behind Troy's chair. The two women were a stark contrast in coloring and demeanor—pale and dark, subdued and vibrant.

"How's Dex doing in med school?" Unaware of Mike's distracted gaze, Michael Sr. asked about Troy's younger brother. Since Mike and Troy had practically grown up together, Dexter Anthony and their grandmother who'd raised the boys were like extended family.

"Long hours. But he's killin' it."

"I knew he would. Jillian wants to know when you're coming over for dinner. More for the games afterward than the food."

"Just give me a time, and I'll be there. And tell her I've been reading the dictionary every night. I'm not losing that word game to her again."

"Will do." The two men shook hands again before his dad nodded to Gina over the top of Troy's head. "You sure you don't want me to stay and give you a ride home?"

"No, sir. Thank you, but you need to get to work. Besides, I've been getting home all by myself for a lot of years now."

"I'll make sure she gets home, Dad."

"Son." Michael traded one last nod with Mike before he left.

There was an awkward moment between the four of them in the congested hallway before

Mike stepped to one side. Gina politely followed suit, giving Troy room to spin his chair around and head back to his patient in the workout room. Frannie quietly excused herself and slipped into her office, leaving Mike and Gina standing side by side with their backs against the wall. The woman didn't even come up to his shoulder. But he appreciated the view of dark waves capping her head and the tight, round bump of her bottom farther down.

One by one, doors closed behind Frannie, Troy and Mike's dad. The second her potential boss had gone and they were alone, Gina turned on him. "I didn't ask you to be my chauffeur."

Forget the raw attraction simmering in his veins. Her hushed, chiding tone gave Mike an idea of what the next few weeks were going to be like, and it wasn't going to involve fun or easy. But he'd been rising to one challenge or another his entire life. Five feet and a few inches or so of attitude wasn't about to scare him off. She might as well get used to how he intended to run things with her. "You didn't ask me to be your physical therapist, either. But it looks like *that's* going to happen." He took her into his office and closed the door. "Have a seat. I need to do an informal assessment before we get started."

She eyed the chair where she'd sat earlier, and obstinately remained in place. "I've already had two evaluations, three if you count the orthopedist who sent me to PT in the first place."

"Well, none of them reported to me, and I've got no paperwork on you, so have a seat." Mike sat and pulled up a new intake file on his computer screen.

She poked a finger at the corner of his desk. "Listen, Choir Boy. Your father outranks me and can give me orders. But you can't."

Choir Boy? What happened to *Catnip*?

And why couldn't the woman just call him Mike? "Fine. Stand. I'm still asking questions."

He typed in her name as she snatched her hand away. "Are you making fun of me now? You don't know me. You don't know my life."

If he recalled correctly, he'd saved that life.

"Age? Address? Phone number? Surgeon?" He typed in the answers as she rattled them off. "What are your goals?"

She puffed up like a banty hen, swearing a couple of words in Spanish, before perching on the chair across from him. "My goals? Isn't it obvious? I want to be a cop again. And not just some face sitting behind a desk, either. I want to be able to pick up my gun and take down a perp and be the first Latina on one of your father's SWAT teams."

"You want me to put in a good word for you?" He met her gaze across the desk. "You're going to have to earn that. I warn you, Dad and I are close, but he doesn't let anybody tell him what to do when it comes to the job." Mike leaned back in his chair. "But I have a feeling you're familiar with that kind of attitude."

"Are you trying to make me angry?"

"Apparently I don't have to work very hard at it."

Her eyes widened and the tight lines around her mouth vanished. "Things have been a little tense…" She parted her lips to continue, closed them again, processed a thought, then leaned forward to ask. "Can you make me whole again? If I can't be a cop, I don't know… My family is counting on me… I'm used to dealing with problems myself. But this…" She tilted her chin, as if the proud stance could erase the vulnerability that had softened everything about her for a few moments. "I need this to happen."

In other words, *Rescue me.* He'd just taken a hit to his Achilles' heel. Not that this woman looked like she wanted a knight in shining armor, but a woman in need had always been a problem for Mike. Caroline had needed him to build her confidence and stand up to her parents. Frannie had needed him to feel safe. They weren't the first, and he had a feeling they wouldn't be the last. Maybe it had something to do with atoning for the mistakes of his rebellious youth after his mother had died of cancer. Maybe it had something to do with finding a purpose for his life the day he helped rescue his stepmother, Jillian, and Troy from a bomber. Maybe it had something to do with that lonesome need to be needed—to be the one man that a woman had to have in her life.

And maybe he *was* too hardheaded to accept defeat because he heard himself saying, "I can help it happen if you let me. You're going to have to take orders from someone besides my dad. Can you do that? Do what I tell you? *Not* do more than I tell you?" he emphasized, suspecting that *slow* and *easy* weren't in Gina's vocabulary. "You can do as much damage by pushing too hard too soon as the original injury inflicted."

"I can do more than those other therapists were letting me. I can handle pain. And training is something I've done in sports since middle school, and certainly at the police academy. I'll do my job if you do yours."

Not exactly the clear-cut agreement he'd been looking for. But he'd take it. If Gina saw this as a competition, he'd give her a run for her money—and then make sure she won. He reached across the desk with his right hand, purposely challenging her to respond with the hand that rested limply in the sling.

A light flashed in her eyes, like a sprinkling of sugar dissolving in rich, warm coffee. Not the sour kind Frannie made, either. Then she thrust her hand out of the end of the sling. Her thumb and forefinger latched on to his hand with a decent grip, but the last three fingers simply batted against the back of his knuckles. Mike stretched each limp finger back, checking the muscle tone, before he finished the informal assessment and gave her hand a reassuring squeeze. Then he pulled away and pushed to his feet. "You accept that I'm in charge of your recovery? That when it comes to your health, I'm the boss?"

He towered over her, but there wasn't any backing down to this woman. Gina stood as well, adjusting her arm in the sling. "You want to be the boss, Choir Boy? Let's do this."

An hour later, she had a sheen of perspiration dotting her forehead and neck, and her left arm was shaking with the extra exertion of compensating for her damaged right shoulder and weak arm. Mike had a pretty good idea of why Gina had run into issues with her previous physical therapists. The woman was as fit as any athlete he'd ever worked with, and her frustration with the limited use of her hand and arm was obvious. Her assessment session had been a battle of wills, with Gina determined to perform any task Mike asked of her, even when the purpose of the exercise was to give him a clear idea of her limitations.

His dad had been right. Gina's recovery was going to be a mental challenge as much as a physical one. He walked her to the door, suggesting she wear something besides jeans for the next session and giving her a list of dos and don'ts for her recovery.

Since he'd been raised to be a gentleman, he lifted the denim jacket hanging from her left wrist as she struggled to put it on and slipped it up her arm before tucking it securely around her healing shoulder. He wasn't sure if that grunt was a protest of independence or a flash of pain. It certainly wasn't a *thank you*. Still, he helped her pull the ends of her hair from beneath the collar, sifting the damp waves through his fingers and learning their silky texture before he leaned in to whisper, "You're welcome." She grunted a second time, and Mike chuckled as he reached around her to push open the door and follow her out into the sunshine that warmed the springtime air. "How are you going to get home?"

She eyed the scattering of cars in the parking lot, between the reclaimed warehouses that had been converted into various businesses and lofts, and the busy street beyond. "If there's no snow on the ground, I can walk."

Mike thumbed over his shoulder at his black pickup truck. "I'll give you a ride."

"You're going to leave work in the middle of the day to drive me home?"

The gusting breeze blew her hair across her cheek, and he curled his fingers into his palms against the urge to touch those dark waves again. "It's not that far. My next appointment isn't until after lunch. Troy can cover any emergencies that crop up."

"Therapist, not chauffeur," she reminded him.

"Suit yourself. I'll see you tomorrow?"

"I'll be here."

"No working out between now and then, understand? You can do the hand exercises, but no running and no lifting weights."

She smoothed the fluttering hair behind her ear and held it in place there. "What about the yoga stretches?"

"Lower half of your body? Sure. But nothing that could create a balance issue. If you fall and catch yourself with that arm, you'll set your recovery back another two weeks, if not permanently."

"Understood." She stepped off the sidewalk and headed across the parking lot.

"Really?" he challenged. Promising to obey his directives was different from hearing the words and understanding them.

Her sigh was audible as she turned back to face him. "Are you always this stubborn?"

"You bring it out in me."

"I won't apologize for being a strong woman."

"I wouldn't want you to." However, that acceptance and respect needed to go both ways. "I won't apologize for being a nice guy."

"Who says you're—?"

"'Choir Boy'?"

She snapped her lips shut on the next retort, perhaps conceding that he knew exactly what the reverse prejudice of that nickname meant to her. Nice guys didn't cut it in her world. Too bad she hadn't known him back in the day. Of course, teenage bad-boy reputation aside, if he hadn't gotten his act together, he might still be in a wheelchair or even dead. He sure wouldn't have sobriety, a college degree, his own business, nor would he be in a position to help her.

He watched the debate on what she should say next play over her features. *That's right, sweetheart. There's a difference between nice and naive.* "My apologies, Mr. Cutler."

Without so much as a smile, she turned and walked out to the street, where she changed direction to follow traffic along the sidewalk toward the lights and crosswalk at the corner. Fine. So friendship wasn't going to happen between them anytime soon. And those curious, lustful urges she triggered in him were never going to be assuaged. But maybe, just maybe, they could learn how to get along.

Mike tucked his hands into the pockets of his gray nylon running pants. He mentally calculated how many blocks she'd have to walk and how many busy streets she'd have to cross before she got home. He'd cover two or three times that distance on his morning runs. But he didn't have two recent gunshot wounds or the muscle fatigue of a therapy session to slow him down. She'd be on her feet for another thirty minutes before she got the chance to rest.

Maybe he should have insisted on driving her home. He fingered the keys in his pocket, wondering how much Gina would protest if he pulled up beside her and…

That was weird.

Mike's eyes narrowed as Gina's steps stuttered and she suddenly darted toward the curb. She pulled up sharply, swiveling her gaze, looking everywhere except straight back at him. Mike's balance shifted to the balls of his feet. Had she seen or heard something that had alarmed her? Maybe she'd simply recognized a familiar face driving past.

Gina dodged a pair of businesswomen hurrying by in their suits and walking shoes, clearly unaware of whatever had caught her attention. Three more pedestrians passed her before she shook her head, as if dismissing what she'd seen or heard, and turned toward the intersection again.

By that time, Mike was already across the parking lot, jogging toward her. He fell into step about a half block behind her, following her through the intersection before the traffic light changed. Although the number of pedestrians heading to work or running to the periodic transit stops to catch the next city bus filled the sidewalk between them, he had no problem keeping Gina in sight, simply because of his height.

Her posture had subtly changed after that original reaction. There was less of the defiance she'd shown him at the clinic and more of a wary alertness. Judging by the occasional glimpses of either cheekbone, he could see she was scanning from side to side as she walked. Who was she looking for? What had she seen or heard that put her on guard like that?

She pulled out her cell phone, glancing over her left shoulder at the traffic as she placed a call, before Mike noticed what might have gotten her attention. A tan luxury sedan zipped across two lanes before it slowed dramatically, pulling even with Gina and matching her pace. He moved toward the curb, trying to read the license plate of the car. Other vehicles ran up behind the car, then swerved around it. He quickened his own pace to see the silhouette of a ball cap above the driver's seat headrest. That wasn't any little old lady driving it, poking along at her own pace. Was that car following Gina?

And then Mike saw something that hastened his feet into a dead run. The driver raised his arm over the passenger seat, his fingers holding a gun. "Gina!"

She spun around. The instant he shouted her name, the driver floored it, swinging into the next lane, darting around a bus and speeding through a yellow light. Horns honked, brakes screeched.

Mike snaked his arm around Gina's waist, lifting her off her feet and hauling her away from the car. At the last second, he could see the driver hadn't held a weapon, after all, but had made that crass gesture with two outstretched fingers and a flick of his thumb, imitating firing a gun.

"What the hell, Choir Boy?" Gina's phone flew from her grasp, skittering across the sidewalk and getting kicked once before a helpful soul picked it up.

Mike set her down in front of the yellow brick facade of a bail bondsman's office, keeping his body between her and the street. The other man handed Gina her cell phone, pausing to eye Mike suspiciously, as if the guy thought he was assaulting her. Mike's hand was still at Gina's waist, the adrenaline of taking instinctive action to protect her still vibrating through his grip. He nearly bit out a warning for the other guy to move on when Gina smiled and waved him on his way.

Interesting how she managed a polite thank you and a reassurance that she was all right for the young man, but she'd cursed at Mike. Even more interesting how quickly the mix of concern and the remembered sensation of her body snugged against his made him vividly aware of every tight curve of her petite frame. He was so not thinking of her as a patient right now. But the sexual awareness burned through him as quickly as the shove against his chest separated them again. "Let go of me."

"Are you okay?"

"Are you following me?" Her question overlapped his.

"Somebody is." Mike splayed his fingers apart, releasing his grip without giving her space to move away from the wall. Those fractious nerves from his teenage injury tingled through his hips and the small of his back, protesting the abrupt movements and tension running through him. But he ignored the familiar shards of pain. "What the hell is going on?"

Although the casing on her phone was scratched, he could see on the screen between them that her call was still connected. Her focus was there instead of answering his questions. "I'm fine. Just let me do my job." She put the phone back to her ear, reporting a license plate number. "I didn't get the last two digits."

"Thirty-six," Mike answered, reciting the number he'd seen.

Her dark eyes tilted up to his. "Tan Mercedes?" He nodded. "Three six, Derek," she reported into the phone, holding Mike's gaze while she talked. "Yeah, it circled around the block. Let me know what you find out. Thanks." She disconnected the call and tucked the phone into the back pocket of her jeans. "What are you doing here? And don't you ever pick me up like that again."

"I want to know why that guy threatened you."

Her dark eyes narrowed as she studied his face. "Are you hurt?"

Yeah, a sharp twist of a pinched nerve had just made his left thigh go numb, so she must have noticed the tight clench of his jaw. But that injury was old news. He needed to understand what was going on now. "Answer the question."

Dismissing her concern because he had dismissed it, she glanced around him at the next stream of pedestrians getting off the bus and dropped her voice to a terse whisper. "I'm a cop."

Shifting to the side, Mike braced one hand on the bricks beside her head and created a barrier between Gina and anyone who might accidently bump into her shoulder. "You're not in uniform. Either we have some random whack-job roaming the streets of Kansas City or that was personal. Did you recognize him? Is he the man who shot you?"

She put her hand in the middle of his chest to hush him when a couple of people turned their heads and slowed, catching wind of the conversation. "You saw it. The driver was acting suspiciously. I was doing my duty by calling it in." When she tried to dismiss the conversation and move around him, Mike dropped his hand back to the cinch of her waist, refusing to budge. She muttered something in Spanish, then tipped her face up to his. "I was probably staring at him too long, and he mimicked shooting me instead of flipping me off. Thought he was being funny."

Mike wasn't laughing. "Okay, so you're a tough chick. I get that. Didn't anybody ever teach you how to answer a polite question? I grew up around cops—I know the signs of somebody going into alert mode. You're not armed. You're injured. You don't have backup. I'm not going to think any less of you if you tell me that guy spooked you."

Her pinpoint gaze dodged his for an instant, revealing a chink in her armor. Mike summoned every bit of his patience to wait her out before she finally told him something that wasn't a flip-pant excuse, meant to dismiss his concern. "I've seen that car before—driving by my house at night the past couple of weeks. And now…" She curled her fingers into his shirt, pulling him half a step closer as a group of pedestrians strolled behind him. Sure, she was avoiding foot traffic, but she'd also moved him closer to whisper, "Do you remember the vehicle from the shooting?"

"Yeah, but it wasn't a car. Certainly not any-thing top-of-the-line like that. Did you recognize the driver? He could have ditched the truck I saw." Although he doubted the man who owned that piece of junk would also own a Mercedes.

"The man who shot me—I never saw his face."

Mike dipped his head to hear her over the noise of the crowd and traffic. "I thought it might be someone else I'd recognize."

"Like who?"

"My sister's boyfriend. He doesn't like me, and the feeling's mutual. Or one of a group of bikers I ticked off a few weeks back…the day I got shot. That can't be a coincidence, can it?" One thing he had to give Gina credit for—whether she was venting her temper, discussing a case or admitting her fear—she looked him straight in the eye. He had to admire a woman with that kind of confidence. But it also gave Mike a chance to read the real emotions behind her words. "I couldn't see this guy's face, either. He had dark glasses on and a ball cap pulled low over his forehead. I couldn't even give you a hair color or age. I don't suppose you got a description of him?"

She was afraid, and it didn't take a rocket scientist to guess that fear wasn't an emotion she was used to feeling. Mike moved his fingers from her waist to stroke the sleek muscles of her arm, wanting to reassure her somehow. But he had an idea she wasn't used to accepting comfort, either. "No. But you think that car has been following you? Is that why you're running the plate number?"

"My partner is. Technically, I'm on medical leave. He's doing me a favor."

Knowing the shooter was still out there, and

that she wouldn't be able to identify the man if he came back to finish the job until she saw a gun pointed at her would rattle anybody. Even an experienced cop like Gina. "Come back to the clinic. I'll drive you home."

"No." She started to push him away, but the tips of her fingers curled into the cotton knit of his polo, lightly clinging to the skin and muscle underneath. "No, thank you," she added, apologizing for the abruptness of her answer. "It's probably someone who lives or works in the neighborhood. There are gangbangers in my part of town. They know I'm a cop. Maybe one of them recognized me. And maybe it was nothing. After the shooting, I'm overly suspicious of any vehicle that slows down or stops when it shouldn't."

He was surprised to feel her reaching out to him, even more surprised to realize how every cell leaped beneath her touch, even one as casual as her hold on him now. This wild attraction he was feeling was unexpected—and most likely unreciprocated, if his track record for following his hormones and heart was any indication. Gina had had her entire life turned upside down, and she was learning how to cope with the changes. All she needed from him right now was a steady presence she could hold on to for a few seconds while she regrouped. He could give her that. "I wouldn't rationalize away your suspicions, Gina. Sounds to me like survival skills, not paranoia."

Her gaze finally dropped from his to study the line of his jaw. She smiled when she murmured, "Physical therapist, not counselor. *Not* bodyguard."

"How about friend?" he offered. Because this pseudo embrace against the brick wall was starting to feel a lot like something more than a therapist–patient relationship was happening between them.

"Maybe it *is* a little far to walk." But she wasn't asking for a ride. Another bus pulled up behind him, her phone rang and she pulled away to take out her cell and join the line waiting to board the bus. "I'll see you tomorrow morning... Mike."

She paused before his name, as if it was hard to pronounce.

Maybe it was just hard to accept his offer. "Do you need me to pick you up?"

"*Not* my chauffeur." She raised her voice to be heard above the bus's idling engine.

He raised his, too. "I'm not being nice. I'm being practical."

But she was already climbing on, taking her call. Mike backed away as the bus door closed and the big vehicle hissed and growled, spewing fumes that blocked out the spicy scent he was learning to identify as Gina's.

Mike watched the bus chug up to speed and

sail through the intersection before he turned back toward the PT clinic. He scanned the traffic as he walked, trying to spot the car again. Maybe the driver had circled around the block a third time. Maybe the tan sedan was long gone. Maybe it had nothing to do with Gina or the shooting.

Erring on the side of caution, he pulled out his own phone and texted himself the license plate number before he forgot it. He'd ask his dad or one of his buddies at the police department to see what they could find out about the car and its owner.

He hadn't gotten a look at the shooter who'd sped away that day, either. He'd been too focused on helping the cops who'd been wounded. Had the car triggered a memory in Gina's subconscious mind, reminding her of something she'd seen? Or was all that bravado she spouted the protective armor of a woman who'd had her confidence ripped out from under her feet?

Mike wasn't a cop. But he was thinking like one, and he needed answers.

Was the shooter tracking her down, learning her routine so he could come back and finish the job? If so, did that mean the shooting was personal? Not a random attack on cops?

Was Gina still in danger?

What kind of backup did a cop on medical leave have? Maybe she didn't need Mike to protect her. But, injured as she was, without the ability to use her gun, how would the woman protect herself?

Chapter Five

"Not my chauffeur, Choir Boy," Gina insisted, catching the towel Mike tossed her way with her left hand. Slightly breathless after a duel on side-by-side treadmills that she suspected he'd let her win, she dabbed at the perspiration at her neck and at the cleavage of the gray tank top she wore. "I can get to KCPD headquarters on my own."

After a week of physical therapy sessions with Mike Cutler, she had to give him grief, or else he might begin to think his jokes amused her—and that his efforts to be a gentleman and push her toward recovery with the same mix of authority and restraint his dad used at KCPD might result in her actually liking the guy.

At least he had the sense to respect her fitness level. He allowed her to push hard with her legs and left arm, in addition to the far gentler stretches and coordination exercises he did with her right hand and arm. "I suspect your legs are like jelly, so you're not walking. And I can't wait for you to get there by bus. How much time do you think I can spare for you out of my busy day?" he teased. He picked up his own towel to wipe his face. "I'm driving."

Busy day? Gina picked up the sling he'd let her remove before that last running challenge and swung her gaze over to where Troy was working with a retired firefighter with knee issues. She hadn't seen many other patients. And she'd overheard a conversation between Mike and Frannie on Monday about moving money from his personal account to make a payment on an expensive piece of equipment.

They might come from two different worlds, but growing up in suburbia hadn't guaranteed that a person could make ends meet. Still, the fact that he drove into this part of the city from somewhere else and probably lived in a house big enough to stretch out those long, muscular legs of his made her a little jealous. Heck, he no doubt had more bathrooms in that house than any one man could use, while she intended to take a quick shower here so that she wouldn't have to let her workout scent marinate while she waited in line to use the bathtub at home.

His tone grew serious as he sat down on the bench, facing her. "Are you worried about going back to Precinct headquarters? I'd rather evaluate the status of your grip at the shooting range than bring a gun here."

"No. That's fine. While we're there I can check in with my partner—see if there are any developments in the shooting investigation. Not that I can do anything about it officially, but…" Maybe she should take Mike up on his offer of a ride, in case being back in the building where she could no longer work stirred up her frustrations again—or embarrassment if she discovered she was no better at handling a firearm today than she'd been seven weeks ago. She'd hate to be waiting for the bus if she wanted to make a quick escape.

Those piercing blue eyes studied every nuance of her expression, trying to read her thoughts. "But you want to regain a little control over what you're going through?"

Funny how she'd lost control of everything during those few seconds in the street outside Vicki Bismarck's house.

Not funny how well this man could read her fears and insecurities. But she wasn't about to admit those vulnerabilities to Mike or anyone else. Better a chauffeur than a therapist. "All right, then. You can drive me."

He arced an eyebrow, looking as surprised by the one-time concession as she'd meant him to be. But her plan to catch him off guard and stop him from analyzing her emotions backfired when Mike pushed to his feet. Suddenly, she was nose-to-chest with Mike's lanky frame.

His broad shoulders blocked her peripheral vision and she could feel the heat coming off his body. "Give me fifteen minutes to shower and change, and we'll go."

Catnip. She retreated a step when she realized she was inhaling the earthy smells of sweat and soap and man, and savoring the elemental response his scent triggered inside her. "Make it ten," she challenged, denying her body's feminine reaction. "How much time do you think I can spare for you out of my busy day?"

Mike laughed at her mimicking comeback, and she smiled for a moment before mumbling one of her great-uncle's curses and spinning away to march toward the women's locker room. When had his silly sense of humor started rubbing off on her? She wasn't supposed to like a man like Mike Cutler. At least, she wasn't supposed to like him as anything other than a physical therapist and maybe a friend. Besides, she already had enough responsibilities demanding her time and energy. When did she think she was going to squeeze in dating?

Mike was right about one thing. She needed to be in control of her life, in control of her future, again. She'd be smart to ignore any fluttering of her pulse, any urge to laugh at their banter, and that relentless pull to the heat of his body.

"Ten minutes, Choir Boy."

Gina had learned long ago how to get in and

out of the bathroom quickly and came out of
the shower five minutes later, her skin cooled
and fresh, her libido firmly in check. She towel-
dried her hair and finger-combed the chin-length
waves into place before she started to dress. After
the shooting, she'd switched to a front hook bra
and button-up blouses so she could dress herself.
But, though she'd taken Mike's advice and worn
her KCPD sweats for their therapy sessions, she
wasn't about to show up at Precinct headquarters looking like she'd just come from the gym.
It would be hard enough to be there out of uniform, sending the obvious message to her coworkers and superior officers that this was just
a visit. Looking like a bum might also give them
the impression that she wasn't coming back.

But the fitted jeans she took from her bag were
a little tricky when she had to pull them up, especially when her skin was still dewy from the
shower. The twinge in her shoulder and result-
ing tingling in her fingers when she gave them a
tug warned her she needed to swallow her pride
and ask someone to help her. When she heard a
woman's voice out in the locker area, Gina gave
a mental prayer of thanks that she wouldn't have
to leave the locker room with her jeans hanging
on her hips to go get Mike.

"Hey, could you help…?" Gina's question died
when she saw Frannie dabbing at her red-tipped
nose as she folded towels from a laundry bas-

ket and stacked them on a shelf. The woman with hair the color of a penny kept muttering something that sounded like *stupid ninny.* Gina cleared her throat to announce her presence. "Are you okay?"

Frannie spun around, hugging a fluffy towel to her chest. "I'm sorry. Did you need something?"

Gina pointed to her jeans. "I'm stuck."

"Oh, right." Frannie dropped the towel into the basket and hurried over to give the black pants a final tug. "Mike said you needed to be careful with that arm."

"Thanks." Gina took over buttoning the waistband and pulling up the zipper. "I guess I need to stick to sweats." But Frannie had gone back to folding. Maybe this wasn't any of her business, but the woman had just helped her pull up her pants, so there was a bit of a connection there. Moving closer, Gina plucked a hand towel from the basket and held it out to the taller woman. "What happened? And don't say *nothing* because you've been crying for a while."

Frannie took the towel and pulled off her glasses to dry her eyes. "I got a phone call."

"From your ex?" Even the eye that didn't seem to focus looked startled. When the other woman backed away, Gina reached for her hand. "I eavesdrop. I'm a cop. I like to know who the people around me are. You and Troy were arguing about a restraining order for your ex yesterday."

Frannie put her glasses back on and sort of smiled. "We were arguing about Troy's van. He drove me to the judge's office to reinstate the order. Troy can't use his legs, you know, so he has this special van where he uses a hand brake and accelerator to drive. I mentioned one thing about how fast he was going before a jerky stop at a red light, and he started yelling about the van falling apart, and that he hadn't had a chance to clean it up before I rode in it. I thought he was mad at me. I don't deal with confrontation very well."

"Have you ridden with Troy before?"

Frannie shook her head.

Sounded like wounded male pride. She thought she'd detected a few stolen glances between the two coworkers. Maybe Troy wasn't keen on Frannie seeing the extent of his handicap. "Not everyone who argues with you is going to hurt you."

"I know. Troy's usually really sweet and funny. I probably caught him on a bad day." That sounded like a woman who'd been victimized making excuses for a man who'd yelled at her or hurt her.

This whole conversation—and all the other interactions she'd had with the skittish Frannie—reminded her of Vicki Bismarck. She wondered if that last call she'd been working on before the shooting had been resolved. Was Gordon Bismarck still in jail? Had his big brother, Denny, and his friends retaliated against Vicki in any way? Had Vicki gotten the medical treatment she'd needed? Moved in with her sister? Pressed charges against Gordon?

Or were Denny and his biker boys more interested in retaliating against the police officers who'd arrested Gordon? Had he been the man in the rusty SUV the day she'd been shot? Gina's fingers drifted to her right shoulder—not feeling a physical or even phantom pain, but remembering with vivid detail the bullet tearing through her body, the multiple gunshots exploding all around her and the snow soaking up her blood and body heat.

Gina realized she was shivering before she pulled herself from the memories. The Bismarcks weren't her case anymore. And everyone at KCPD was working on finding out who'd shot one of their own. Everyone but her, that is. She wasn't used to being the victim. She didn't like being out of the investigative loop or being taken off the front line of protecting her city, her family and herself.

But the situation right in front of her was one she could handle. Gina sat and patted the bench beside her. She had a feeling Frannie's tears weren't really about the argument with Troy. "Tell me about the phone call."

"From Leo?" Frannie hesitated for a moment before sitting. "I was getting ready for work this morning. I didn't pick up. As soon as I heard his voice, I let it go straight to my machine. He said he missed me. That he still loved me. That he always would." She paused a moment before adding, "He wants to see me."

"Is he supposed to have any contact with you?" When Frannie shook her head, Gina's first instinct was to pull out her own phone and file a report. But she wasn't a cop right now. She couldn't take action, but she could give advice. "Polite or not—even if Leo pulled at your heartstrings—you need to call the police and report it." The jerk had probably just been served with the restraining order and thought he could talk her out of it. "Keep a record of any contact he makes with you—by phone, email, certainly in person. Do you know his parole officer's name? He needs to know about the call, too."

The other woman straightened her shoulders and nodded. "I know that's what I'm supposed to do. I can ask Mike to help. He said his dad was looking into it." Frannie offered Gina a smile that quickly faded. "I'm such a ninny. Have you ever been so scared of a person that you can't even think when he's around?" She stood abruptly and carried the hand towel to the clothes hamper near the shower room. "Look who I'm talking to. You're not scared of anything."

Gina was thinking that never regaining the full use of her hand and arm was a pretty terrifying thing to contemplate. Losing her job. Letting her family down. Never getting the life she wanted for all of them. "Maybe not people," she confessed.

Although there was one faceless shooter who'd put her on guard from the moment she'd regained consciousness in the hospital. Like nearly every other waking moment, Gina wondered if there'd ever be an arrest of the man who'd targeted her and her partner. They weren't on Gordon Bismarck's good side after arresting him. There'd certainly been plenty of time for Denny to switch vehicles and come back to the house to shoot her and Derek. According to Mike, the SUV's plates had been unreadable. A citywide search for a rusted SUV matching the description he'd given the police had turned up nothing useful. Even the license number on the tan sedan she and Mike had seen wasn't any help. The plates were stolen, according to Derek. The car they'd been registered to belonged to an elderly man who rarely drove it and didn't even know the plates were missing.

Could the Bismarck brothers and their friends be running a stolen-car ring? Or even have legitimate access to a variety of vehicles? In her mind, Bobby Estes was a viable suspect, too. She wouldn't put it past Bobby to try something like that. From what she knew of her sister's smarmy boyfriend, his driving a stolen car, or one with a falsified registration and plates like the Mercedes she'd seen following her, wouldn't surprise her. Shooting the woman who stood in the way of getting what he wanted wouldn't surprise her, either.

Surely someone at KCPD had looked into the background of the prime suspects who'd been at the scene right before the shooting or lived in the same neighborhood. She certainly would. If she was on the case. But she wasn't. And until someone else found the answers, identifying a suspect and a motive, the shooter remained at large—and had the advantage of knowing her, while she remained clueless to his face and name and whether he was coming after her to finish the job he'd started.

"I know what fear is." Gina stood when Frannie resumed folding the towels, probably thinking the long pause meant the conversation was over. "You just have to decide you're not going to let it rule your life."

"That's easier said than done."

"I know. You have to keep trying—every day—to be stronger than the fear. If it gets you one day, then you wake up the next and you try harder." Frannie hugged a towel to her chest again and nodded, trying to internalize the hard-won advice that Gina had learned in No-Man's Land. Gina smiled and added a little practical advice to that philosophical wisdom. "If Leo does come to see you, call 9-1-1. If he physically threatens you, fight back. As hard as you can." She gestured as she gave each instruction. "Stomp on his instep. Gouge his eyes. Ram your hand against the bottom of his nose. And, of course, there's always the old goodie—kicking him where it counts." Frannie silently repeated each hand movement. Gina repeated them for her, encouraging her to use more force. "Scream your head off, too. Help will come running. At least around here. Either Troy or Mike has his eyes on you whenever I'm here. Probably when I'm not, too. Those two have a good-guy streak in them a mile wide."

Frannie nodded. "I know. They've been through so much, and they're still so nice. Any girl would be lucky to..." Her cheeks turned pink as she swallowed whatever emotion she'd been about to share. "Mike's like a big brother to me."

Gina wasn't forgetting where this conversation had started. "And Troy?"

Frannie's blush intensified. Interesting. Maybe she wasn't so keen on Troy seeing her shortcomings, either. "They're the best. I'll talk to Mike and call Leo's parole officer." She divvied up the clean towels and put half away before carrying the basket to the locker room door. She paused there, looking to Gina before repeating her advice. "Feet. Eyes. Nose. Family jewels."

Gina grinned. "And scream like crazy."

"Thanks."

For what? All she'd done was give the woman a few tools to use if she ever needed to defend herself against her ex. It was what any cop would do. Acknowledging that it felt good to do something that made her feel useful again, Gina quickly finished dressing. No doubt Mike would have some comment about missing her ten-minute challenge to be ready. He'd expect her to laugh. And if she wasn't careful, she probably would.

They've been through so much...

What had Frannie meant by that comment? What could Troy and Mike, especially Mike, have endured that would make the other woman sound surprised—almost awestruck—that the two men would end up being such nice guys? Such hero figures to her?

And why was Gina so curious to find out the answer to that question?

"I'D LIKE TO check in with my partner first." Gina stepped into the elevator and pushed the 3 button on the panel, taking her and Mike upstairs instead of down to the shooting range in the basement. "Our desks..." Hopefully hers hadn't been filled yet, but she knew her partner had been temporarily reassigned to ride with someone else until she could get back to patrol duty. "Derek's desk," she corrected, "is on the third floor." She checked the time on her phone before tucking it into her back pocket. "They're probably getting out of morning roll call about now."

"Not a problem. My schedule's flexible." Mike joined her at the back railing. "Today is all about taking your recovery to the next level. Making that hand usable again."

Gina inhaled a deep breath. "I hope there's a level after that. *Usable* doesn't sound like it'll get me the job I want."

"The healing part I can't control. But I'll teach your body to do everything it's capable of. I promise. It's just a matter of time and training." Even leaning against the car's back wall, Mike was a head taller than she was.

Gina was used to being shorter than most men, often shorter than anyone in the room except for her great-aunt. But her bulky uniform vest, gun and determined attitude usually beefed up her presence. Yet there was something about Mike Cutler that seemed to fill up the limited space of the elevator and make her feel tiny, fragile, more feminine than usual. Perhaps it was the lack of the uniform and gear she usually wore. Or perhaps it was the protective way he opened doors for her and stood on her right side, shielding her injured arm now that she didn't have to wear the sling around the clock anymore. Although she might be vertically challenged, Gina had never considered herself delicate in any way. Not since she was a child had she needed anyone to protect her. Back then, an absent father and an ailing mother had forced her to grow some tough emotional armor and learn to fight and stay smarter than any adversary. Gina took care of herself and her family all on her own. She didn't need a man taking care of her.

Even if he did smell good and generate the kind of heat she fantasized about on chilly spring mornings like this.

"Am I your only patient today?" she asked, needing to start a conversation before she did something damsel-like and leaned into that body heat.

He tucked his fingers into the pockets of his jeans and answered. "Yeah. Business has been slow."

She wasn't blind to the lack of company at the CAPT Center in the mornings. "You didn't exactly pick the most lucrative area of the city to set up shop. Have you ever thought of affiliating with a hospital? Even moving the center a couple of blocks over to Westport would make it appealing to a broader audience. Not everyone feels safe spending a lot of time that close to No-Man's Land. You know, that part of the city where urban renewal hasn't quite reached—"

"I know what No-Man's Land is. Son of a cop, remember?" He tilted his face down to hers. "I've done the hospital thing. We're exactly where we want to be, offering physical therapy services to an underserved part of the city. We're our own bosses now. Troy grew up in the neighborhood, and I've had my share of experience there."

"Your share of experience?" Gina scoffed. "You're telling me you've been on the mean streets of the city? You've broken the law? I pegged you for a middle-class suburbia guy all the way."

Was that a scowl? Did Mr. Good Guy have a secret sore spot she'd just poked? He straightened away from the railing. "I'm not the *choir boy* you think I am. I've done things."

"Like what? Cheat on a test? Run a red light?"

The scowl deepened. Gina felt a stab of guilt, thinking back to Frannie's comment about Mike going through something terrible in his past. Had her smart mouth just crossed a line?

"You don't live in the suburbs? Have enough land that you can't touch your house and the neighbor's at the same time?" Good grief. Was she actually making light of the topic to try and restore that goofball smile to his face? "I was really hoping you had three bathrooms because I was totally going to come for a visit and spend the afternoon soaking in one of those tubs."

She heard an exhale of breath that sounded like a wry laugh.

"You want to get in my bathtub?" There was the glimpse of white teeth amid the sexy dusting of his beard. His voice dropped to a throaty whisper as he leaned in. "I wouldn't object to that."

Gina couldn't remember the last time she'd blushed hard enough to feel heat in her cheeks. "I meant…our house is small. I share one bathroom with four… I can't take my time…" She growled at her flummoxed reaction to his teasing innuendo.

Not a boyfriend. *Not* a lover. *Not* a man who should be getting under her skin.

Thankfully the elevator doors slid open, and she could escape the sound of Mike's laughter.

But she never got the chance to get her armor fully in place again. A trio of SWAT cops waited just outside the elevator, greeting Mike with a chorus of "Mikey," handshakes and a ribbing about an upcoming barbecue contest.

Gina knew the three officers, dressed in solid black, except for the white SWAT logo she coveted embroidered on their chest pockets. These were her trainers. Members of KCPD's elite SWAT Team One, led by Captain Cutler. The one with the black hair, Sergeant Rafe Delgado, was even slated to lead the new tactical team she wanted to be a part of.

Clearly, they were all longtime friends, with Mike giving the jokes right back, teasing Holden Kincaid, the team's sharpshooter, about the dogs living at his house who were all smarter than him. He asked about Sergeant Delgado's son, Aaron, and pointed to the baby bump just beginning to show on the woman with the long ponytail, Miranda Gallagher. "They're not letting you out into the field, are they, Randy?"

Gina admired the tall blonde who had been KCPD's first female SWAT officer. She'd shared a couple of private conversations with Gina about the challenges and rewards of being a woman with her specialized training. Officer Gallagher cradled her hand against her belly. "For now, these bozos are letting me drive the van. Pretty soon, though, I'll be relegated to equipment maintenance, and then it's maternity leave."

Gina felt like an afterthought, and considered ducking back into the elevator with the two detectives who snuck in behind her to go downstairs. She hadn't even realized she'd been backing away from the animated reunion until she felt Mike's hand at the small of her back, pulling her forward to stand beside him. "You all know Gina Galvan, right?"

Sergeant Delgado nodded. "Of course, we know our star recruit. We miss you at training."

Holden agreed. "She keeps us on our toes."

"Hi, Gina." Miranda Gallagher smiled down at her.

Apparently, she was going to be a part of this conversation after all. "Officer Gallagher."

Miranda tilted her head. "We talked about that."

Gina nodded. "Randy."

Sergeant Delgado pointed to her arm. "I heard you were at Mike's clinic. How's the recovery going?"

"Fine." She glanced up at Mike. *Was* she getting any better?

Mike's hand rubbed a subtle circle beneath her denim jacket, and she nearly startled at the unexpected tendrils of warmth webbing out across her skin and into the muscles beneath. "She's progressing nicely. Slowly but surely, I'm seeing improvement every day."

"That's good to hear." Holden tapped his thigh. "You willing to give out some free advice to the guy who once saved your life?"

Saved his life?

"What's up?" Mike asked. "And I thought I saved myself."

Saved himself? *I'm not the* choir boy *you think I am, Gina. I've done things.* She still couldn't get her head around what kind of secrets a guy like Mike might have.

"You wish," Holden teased before getting serious. "My knee hasn't been right since I took a tumble off a roof doing sniper duty last week. Anything I can do besides load up on ibuprofen?"

"You should go to Mike's clinic." Gina wasn't sure where the suggestion had come from, other than a deep-seated need to keep things even between them. If Mike was supporting her in a moment of social discomfort, then she'd support him. "The location's not that far from headquarters. You could stop in over lunch or right after work."

"I'll do that." Holden smiled at Gina. "He's obviously doing something right with you, so that's a good recommendation."

Mike's fingers pressed into her back. The tension flowing from him into her didn't exactly feel like a thank you. "Call for an appointment. My assistant will make sure we squeeze you in."

"I'll do that. Thanks."

Sergeant Delgado checked his watch and hurried the conversation along. "I hate to break up the party, but we've got an inspection this morning. We'd better get down to the garage and secure the van."

"Good to see you guys."

"You, too, Mikey."

There was another round of handshakes, and a hug with Miranda before the three uniformed officers got on the elevator and Mike pulled Gina aside to whisper, "I don't need you to drum up business for me."

"And I don't need you to stand up for me."

He shrugged. "It's what people do. Make everyone feel included. What is your hang-up with me being nice to you?"

She propped her hands at her hips and tilted her face to his. "You know those are my superior officers, right? I shouldn't be socializing with them."

"I practically grew up with those guys. That was running into family, not socializing."

"You weren't including me in the conversation to curry favor with them, were you? I want to earn my spot on the new team on merit, not because I'm friends with the captain's son."

Suddenly, the hushed argument was over. He straightened. "So, we're friends now? And here I thought you were going to fight me every step of the way."

She stared at his hand when he reached for hers, overriding the instinctive urge to close the short distance and lace her fingers together with his. No, she couldn't start leaning on Mike just because he made it so easy to do so.

Gina heard a wry chuckle, although she didn't see a smile, as he curled his fingers into his palm and turned toward the desk sergeant's station to check in and get visitor badges. "Right. Just friends. Come on. Let's find your partner."

Chapter Six

"Did you talk to the man who had his plates stolen?" Gina asked, scrolling through the sketchy details of the report on Derek's computer screen. Had he always been this lax about following up with paperwork on the calls they handled? Had she been too obsessive about her own A+ work ethic to notice his borderline incompetence? Or was he skating by on minimal effort without her at his side every day to push him into being the best cop he could be? "Could you tie him to the Bismarck brothers or Bobby Estes?"

Derek perched on the corner of his desk, looking over her shoulder at the screen. "It was just me running a plate for you. I didn't follow up because there wasn't any crime."

Gina shook her head, closing down the page. At least a mouse was easy to control with just her thumb and index finger. It wasn't frontline action, but she could make herself useful doing a little research. "Um, theft? Maybe tell one of the detectives working that stolen-car ring? You know I think Bobby is involved with something like that. How else could he afford the different cars he drives? And, clearly, Denny Bismarck is a motor head. You saw that bike he was riding. Does he work in auto repair? A guy like that could easily lift plates off another vehicle."

Speaking of detectives, her gaze slid across the maze of desks and cubicles to spot Mike chatting with a plainclothes officer she recognized as one of the department's veterans, Atticus Kincaid. Was he related to Holden Kincaid, the SWAT sharpshooter? From senior officers down to the administrative assistant in the chief's office, they'd all said hi or waved or nodded or smiled. He was a law-enforcement legacy more at home at Precinct headquarters because of his father's seniority than she was after six years of scratching her way up through the ranks. If she needed any more evidence that they came from different parts of the city, from virtually two different worlds, that comfortable-in-his-own-skin, one-of-the-boys conversation was it.

"You're right." Derek interrupted thoughts that felt melancholy rather than envious, as she would have had seven weeks ago. Either Mike had social skills she could never hope to possess or she truly was an outsider fighting to find her place among an elite group of cops. "I did mention it to a detective."

Gina spun the chair to face her partner. "What did they say?"

Derek shrugged his broad shoulders. "I just gave him the message."

Gina combed her fingers through her hair and clasped the nape of her neck, biting down on her frustration. "Well, has there been any progress on the shooting investigation?"

Surely, he'd be right on top of the case that was so personal for both of them. He nodded, moving off the desk to open the bottom drawer and pull out a file folder. "Detective Grove and his partner brought Denny Bismarck and his biker buddies in for questioning. Other than the verbal threats they made at the house, we can't get them on anything. They all alibi each other. Said they left the Bismarck house and went straight to the Sin City Bar."

"Can anyone at the bar confirm that?" Gina picked up a notepad and copied names and contact information. Holding a pen was a skill she'd worked on with Mike. The handwriting wasn't pretty, but it was legible, and learning these details was making her feel like a cop again.

"You'd have to ask Grove. Whatever he found out is in that file."

"You didn't follow up?"

"I was in the hospital."

"I know. But after that?"

"No."

"Four suspects accounting for each other's whereabouts is hardly a solid alibi. And that wasn't the first time we stopped Gordon Bismarck from hurting his ex-wife. What if that call was a setup to get us shot all along?"

"What's with all the questions?" he snapped, lowering his voice when the officers at the nearby desks looked his direction. "Look, G, I'm not trying to be a detective. My goal is SWAT."

"Your goal should be being the best cop you can be." Gina stood, tucking the notes into the pocket of her jeans. There had to be something else going on here. "Don't you want to find out who shot you? I want to see that guy behind bars."

"I just want to put it behind me." Derek skimmed his hand over the top of his light brown hair, a look of anguish lining his face. "I can't solve the case for you. Hell, G, I don't remember anything of that afternoon after being shot. The doctors said I hit my head. I remember getting shot, going down, and then…" He shook his head, his frustration evident. "You're not the only one who lost something that day."

"Why didn't you tell me?" She squeezed her hand around his forearm, offering the support she hadn't realized he needed. "I'm so sorry. I didn't know. I'm not criticizing. You must be as frustrated as I am. But I want answers. Justice. For both of us."

"I know." Derek patted her hand. "I didn't want to do anything that would get Vicki hurt either, so I kind of let things slide."

"Vicki Bismarck?" Gina frowned as she remembered a detail from the moments before they'd been shot. "You two were calling each other by your first names that day. Is there something personal going on between you two?"

He shrugged and pulled away to shuffle some papers on his desk. "We may have gone out a couple of times. Nothing came of it."

"You dated a victim you met on a call? A domestic-violence victim? Was that before or after someone tried to end us?"

"Vic is really sweet. Once you get past the shyness."

Gina's mouth opened. Shut. Opened again. "Derek—you know what a jealous idiot Gordon Bismarck is. Going out with his ex-wife could have been the motive to make him go ballistic and target us."

Derek spun around, his tone hushed but angry. "We don't know if that's what happened."

Gina pushed the papers back to the desktop, wanting some concrete answers. "Did you follow up on Gordon? Find out if he saw the two of you together?"

"No. And if I make a stink of it, he might take it out on her."

"Does Vicki mean something to you?"

"I haven't seen her since that day. Let it go, G."

"I'm not blaming you, especially if you're trying to protect her. I just want answers. I want to put someone away for trying to end our lives. Don't you?"

"Sure." Derek dropped his head to stare at the spot where her hand rested on his desk beside his. "Don't you think I feel guilty? I don't remember enough about what happened that day to ID the guy—and now you're suggesting I may have triggered the incident in the first place? I just thought some crazy was targeting cops."

And maybe that *was* the answer. But how could he not be using every spare moment to find the truth? Would guilt, amnesia and worry about a victim's well-being be enough to stop her from pursuing every possible lead?

The telephone on his desk rang. He inhaled a steadying breath before picking up after the second ring. "Officer Johnson. What? Right now? Just what I need," he muttered sarcastically. "No, that's fine."

"Is something wrong?" she asked once he'd hung up.

Derek smoothed the long black sleeves of his uniform and straightened his belt. "Let's drop this conversation for now, okay? I've got a visitor. They're sending him back." He made an apologetic face. "Fair warning."

"Huh?"

And then she understood the cryptic comment. A man wearing a visitor's badge, looking like a hippie version of Derek, with faded jeans, a stained fringed jacket and a graying, stringy ponytail hanging down the middle of his back, came around the cubicle wall. "Dad? What are you doing here?"

"There's my boy." The two shook hands before Harold Johnson pulled Derek in for a black-slapping hug. When he pushed away, he was grinning down at Gina. "Senorita Galvan. What are you doing here?"

Gina remembered the ruddy cheeks, leathered skin and inappropriate comments from her earlier encounters with Derek's father. All the years he'd spent outdoors working at a junkyard between stays in jail or rehab seemed to be aging him quickly but hadn't put a dent in his oily charm. "It's *Officer* Galvan, Harold. Or Gina. Remember?"

"My apologies. But you remind me so much of that *chica bonita* who used to serve me tequila shots at Alvarez's outside Fort Bliss." He chuckled at the memory of the pretty girl who used to wait on his table. "And she was just as insistent I call her Senorita."

Derek shook his head at the tired old joke. "You said that was because she didn't want you calling her after hours."

Harold swatted Derek on the shoulder and told

him to get a sense of humor. "Forgive an old man. I know it's not politically correct, but some habits are hard to change. Come here, honey."

Honey? Like that was any better. Gina went stiff as the older man leaned in for an unexpected hug.

"I'm just glad you and my boy are okay. Scariest moment of my life was when I got that phone call that he'd been shot. I'm glad his mama didn't live to see…"

A hand came over Gina's shoulder, palming Harold's chest and pushing him out of the hug and out of her space. "Easy. She's injured."

Gina didn't need to hear Mike's low voice to know who'd rescued her from the unwanted squeeze. She recognized his scent and the heat of his body against her back. Her breath came out in a huff of relief. She hadn't even been thinking about her rebuilt shoulder. She'd been bothered by the same overly familiar discomfort she got when Derek talked about her sister, Sylvie, as if he wanted to date her. But, not wanting to insult her partner's father and drive a rift between her and Derek, she was glad for the physical excuse. "Sorry, Harold. I've got to watch the arm while it's still healing."

He settled for a loose handshake that extended the awkward moment when he pointed out her limp fingers. "That's too bad about your hand. I guess you didn't see the man who shot you, either. Derek had his back to him but said you were facing him."

Pulling away, Gina tucked her hand inside her jacket against her stomach, surprised by the indirect accusation. Of course, a father would want his child to be safe. Even if that child was a grown man, a good father would want to know why his son had gotten hurt. "I heard the shots. I didn't see—"

"Of course you didn't. Otherwise, you would have warned my boy. He wouldn't have gotten hurt."

"Dad," Derek warned.

Mike moved to Gina's side, positioning his body in a way that forced Harold back another step. He was shielding her again, even as he thrust out his hand. "I'm Mike Cutler."

Harold's bushy brows knotted with confusion as they shook hands. "Harold Johnson. I'm Derek's daddy. You a cop?"

"I'm a friend. And you're out of line."

Derek finished the introductions with an embarrassed sigh. "This is Captain Cutler's son, Dad."

"You're Captain Cutler's boy?" *Boy* wasn't a term Gina would ever use to refer to Mike, especially when he was a solid wall of defense between her and any perceived threat or insult as he was now. Harold's frown at Mike's intrusion flipped into a beaming smile. "I see the resemblance now. Your daddy's got my boy on a short list for his new SWAT team. That means a promotion and more money."

"Gina mentioned it." Mike nodded to Derek. "Congratulations. My dad doesn't make decisions lightly. I understand he's narrowed it down to ten good candidates."

Harold tilted his head to offer Gina a sympathetic frown. "Looks like it's down to nine, unfortunately."

"Harold," Gina chided, "Captain Cutler isn't making his final decision for another week. I have every intention of giving your son and everyone else a run for their money. And I'm as much a victim of that shooting as Derek was."

"Ooh, touched a nerve there, didn't I?" Harold laughed, elbowing Derek's arm before apologizing. "I'm sorry, honey. I just assumed—"

"'I'm sorry, *Officer* Galvan,'" she corrected with the most precise articulation her subtle accent allowed. How had Derek grown up to have any charm at all with a father who didn't possess an ounce of empathy or respect for personal boundaries?

Harold retreated a step as Mike leaned toward him. "Watch your mouth, Johnson."

But Derek had it handled. After sliding Gina an apologetic look, he pulled his father around the corner of the desk. "Why are you here, anyway? What do you need?"

"A place we can talk in private? Family business." Derek seemed relieved to usher his father toward an interview room. "I've been talkin' to a lawyer…"

That's when she discovered she'd latched on to the back of Mike's shirt. Tightly enough to feel the flex of muscle through the cotton knit. Had she really thought Mr. Nice Guy was going after Harold and she'd have to stop him? Or had she subconsciously realized she needed the anchor of his solid presence to get through this difficult visit to Precinct headquarters after all?

She quickly released him and tilted her face to meet Mike's sharp blue gaze when he turned. "You ready to go?"

Gina patted her pocket with the folded notes. "I got enough information that I can follow up a few leads myself."

He arched an eyebrow that was as sleekly handsome as Harold's had been a bushy mess. "Need I remind you that you're on medical leave?"

"It doesn't hurt to make a few phone calls."

"What if you stir up the wrong kind of interest—like that driver who threatened you last week? What if he's the shooter, trying to figure out whether you recognize him? If you start poking the bear, he might stop the next time and finish what he started. You don't have a gun or a badge right now."

"You don't have to remind me of *that*," she snapped, turning toward the elevators. He followed in that long, loose stride that forced her to take two steps for every one of his to beat him to the elevator's call button. "I can't stand by and do nothing. I can at least make a pest of myself with the detectives investigating the shooting."

They had to wait long enough that logic had the chance to sneak past Gina's flare of temper. Mike was right about starting something she couldn't finish. What if she did manage to identify the man who'd shot her? She wouldn't be able to do anything more than call someone else at KCPD to make the arrest. If she confronted him herself, she'd be at a disadvantage. She hadn't been able to protect her partner back when she'd been at 100 percent. What did she think she could do now? Not only could he hurt her again, he could hurt the people around her—her family, innocent bystanders, this tall drink of annoyingly right catnip standing beside her—and she couldn't do anything to stop him.

She was worse than useless as a cop right now. She might well be a danger to everyone around her.

The elevators were busy enough that Gina and Mike were standing there when Derek came around the corner of the last cubicle wall, pulling his father by the arm, hurrying him toward the exit. Whatever *family business* Harold had wanted to discuss, it wasn't going over well with Derek. Words like *lawsuit* and *easy money* popped out of the hushed argument. Was he suggesting that Derek sue the department? The city? Her? To make a profit off getting shot?

Although she was getting used to Mike positioning himself between her and anyone who might accidentally bump into her arm, his protective stance couldn't stop Harold from tugging free of his son's grip and addressing her. "Talk some sense into my boy, *chica*. Do the right thing."

"What are you talking about?"

"Leave her out of this, Dad. You've embarrassed me enough with your get-rich quick schemes. I'm sorry, G. Are we good?"

Gina nodded. Derek was her partner and a friend. He needed her support—not someone grilling him for answers or blaming him for whatever nutso scheme his dad had come up with.

"Come on." Derek snatched Harold by the shoulder of his jacket and pushed him toward the stairwell door. He shoved the door open and pulled his father inside, for privacy to continue the argument as much as the apparent need for speed in making an exit.

She was still staring after them when the elevator arrived and Mike's hand at the small of her back nudged her inside. She crossed to the back of the car and leaned against it, feeling her energy ebbing from the unexpected emotional onslaught of this morning's visit to the Precinct building. "That man is stuck in the Dark Ages. I suspect feminism and ethnic equality aren't part of his vocabulary."

"Derek's dad?"

"The only other Hispanic woman he knows is a bartender from a cantina during his army days? That's how he thinks of me? He blames me for Derek getting shot. No way could a *little woman*, much less one from my part of town, be a good cop and a good partner who could protect his son."

Mike pushed the button for the basement level before resting his hip against the back railing beside her. "He got to you. You don't blame yourself for getting shot, do you?"

Did she? Gina shook off the misguided guilt. "No. I know there's only one person to blame— a wannabe cop killer I can't identify."

"But Johnson made you *feel* guilty." The elevator lurched as it began its descent. "From the way that conversation started, I assumed he must always be a jerk and you were accustomed to blowing him off."

"Usually, I do. But…" Her mood descended right along with the elevator. "I feel out of step here today. Like I don't belong anymore. I don't know the facts of the most important cases. I can't maintain a conversation with people I've worked with for six years. Harold is always going to say something that gets under my skin, but I try to be civil about correcting him for Derek's sake. Yet today, I let him get to me. For a few seconds there, I thought you were going to do what I wanted to."

"Punch him in the mouth?" Gina groaned at his deadpan response. Besides lifting her spirits, the heat of his body standing close to hers was comforting, even though she hated to admit it. She watched as he slid his finger across the brass railing until his pinkie was brushing against hers. She couldn't feel that lightest of touches with her fingertip, but she felt the connection deeper inside. She felt his strength, his easy confidence, his caring. "Have you been back to HQ since the shooting?" he asked.

"Only to sign my incident report and fill out some insurance forms in the administrative offices. A few of the guys stopped by the hospital to see how I was doing. But I haven't done much to keep in touch since then. I've just been so focused..." She looked down at their hands, studying the differences in size and strength, the contrasts of male and female, the olive sheen of her skin next to his paler color. Mike Cutler was different from any man she'd ever taken the time to get to know. Not just on the outside. Somehow, her physical therapist had become her friend. A good friend. Her savior had become a trusted confidant who'd seen her at her worst and motivated her to be her best. He was honest and funny and strong in ways that went beyond his obvious athleticism. "I used to go toe-to-toe with those guys. Today, I feel like a rookie. Like I have to prove myself all over again just to keep my badge."

His pinkie brushed over the top of hers and hooked between her fingers, holding on in the subtlest of ways and deepening the connection she felt. "I bet there's not a one of those guys who could handle what you've been through and come back the way you are."

"They're KCPD's best."

"They're men. Men are terrible patients."

"I'm a terrible patient," she admitted.

"Yeah, but you're cute." Mike's voice had dropped to a husky timbre that skittered along her spine.

"*Cute?* No one has ever called me *cute*. Except maybe Harold Johnson." Although she'd never developed her flirting skills the way her sister had, Gina could hear the huskier notes in her own voice. "Strong. Stubborn. Temperamental. But not *cute*."

"I figured you'd punch me if I called you *sexy* or *built like a fine piece of art*. And I don't want you to injure that arm."

Gina felt herself blushing for the second time that day. But with an infusion of Mike's humor and compassion and that delicious heat she craved, she could also feel her strength coming back. "Stick with *cute*, Choir Boy. That may be the best I can do for a while."

"I'll take that bet." Mike slipped his broad hand beneath her smaller one, turning his palm up to meet hers. "Squeeze my hand. Hard as you can."

Gina straightened at the challenge. "Another exercise?"

"I'm warming you up for the shooting range. Just hold on to me." Her thumb and forefinger easily latched on, but she had to concentrate to move the other fingers. She wasn't sure if it was simple gravity or her own effort, but the last three fingers trembled into place, curling against the side of his hand. When she would have pulled away, he tightened his hand around hers. "Do you feel that?"

"I feel the heat coming off your skin." His grip pulsed around hers. Gina straightened as a renewed sense of hope surged through her. "I felt that." His deep blue eyes were watching her excitement, smiling. So was she. "Does that mean I'm getting the sensation back in my fingers? Am I improving?"

He squeezed her hand again. "Baby steps, Gina. I saw you writing with that pen. Picked it up without hesitation. That's definite improvement."

A dose of reality tempered her enthusiasm. "A

gun is going to be a lot heavier than a pen. Losing control of a weapon is far more serious than making a scribble on a page."

One by one, Mike laced his fingers between hers. "My money's on you, Tiger."

He raised her hand to his lips and kissed her knuckles. She gasped at the surprising tickle of his beard stubble brushing across her skin. Were her nerves finding new pathways to bring sensation back to her hand? Or was that flush of warmth heating her blood a sign that Mike was starting to mean more to her than just a friend?

Gina knew the strangest urge to stretch up on her tiptoes and feel the ticklish sensation of his lips on her own. The elevator jostled them as it slowed its descent, and the tiny shake reminded Gina that this man was all kinds of wrong for her. Any relationship was, at this point in her life. But she could appreciate his friendship and support. "You didn't have to defend me against Derek's dad."

"Maybe I was protecting him from you."

A long-absent smile relaxed her lips as she leaned back, letting her shoulder rest against his arm. "You're a good man, Mike Cutler."

He shrugged. "It's what nice guys do."

Chapter Seven

The following Monday afternoon, Gina was back in training. After her regular session at the CAPT clinic, Mike took her back to the Precinct offices for another round at the shooting range. He was a taskmaster, and she loved the challenges he set up for her. Running. Light weights. Flexibility. Although she still didn't believe they had much in common beyond these sessions, she enjoyed the time they were spending together—Mike the physical therapist putting her through her paces, Mike the friend making her laugh, Mike the protector watching her every move to make sure she didn't injure herself, even as he pushed her to do more.

Today, her hard work and his patience were going to pay off. She was going to shoot her gun, instead of merely manipulating the weapon as she had during last week's session. This time Mike was giving her a baseline test to see how much progress she was making toward returning to active duty.

Other than the officer manning the door to the shooting range, she and Mike were alone and could take their time going through the dexterity exercises they'd practiced last week. She cleared and unloaded, then reloaded her gun twice—once using both hands, and a second time that took several frustrating minutes, while Mike held her left hand down on the counter, forcing her to do more of the work with her right. Now, with their noise-cancelling headphones hanging around their necks, Mike picked up her service weapon.

"You're sure you know what you're doing?" she asked. "It's loaded today."

With an efficiency she envied and respected, he demonstrated that he knew exactly what to do with a Glock 9 mil. "I'm the son of a cop and grew up with guns in the house. Dad always made sure my brother and I knew gun safety and how to handle a weapon."

She put on her ear protection when he did and stepped to the side of the booth as he fired off five rounds. And, if she wasn't mistaken at this distance, he placed all but one of the bullets center mass of the target.

"Show-off," she teased, when he caught her staring in openmouthed admiration.

He grinned, unloading the Glock and setting the gun and magazine on the counter. "Your turn."

He pulled her in front of him, in that protective stance that surrounded her with his warmth. But this wasn't an embrace. It was a physical therapist supporting his patient. She needed to focus on her physical training.

Still, it was hard to miss the intimacy of their positions when her hip brushed against his thigh and his arm reached around her to tap the weapon. "I don't want you to fire any rounds yet. Let's practice raising and aiming the weapon."

Before last week, Gina hadn't handled her weapon since an embarrassing fiasco shortly after she returned home from the hospital. She'd thought she could suit up like any ordinary day and resume the chaos of her life without missing another step. But the heavy Glock had slipped from her grip and bounced across her bedroom floor. Thank goodness the safety had been on. That humbling morning when she realized that all of her cop armor, both figurative and literal, had been stripped away from her by a gunshot was the day she started her determined journey to return to the job and to the protector and provider her family needed her to be.

Realizing the extent of her impediment had been a shock to her sense of self that morning. Today, she knew better than to expect a miracle. But she didn't intend to humiliate herself, either.

She'd ask for a little backup before she put her hand on that weapon again. Crossing her fingers, she raised them to her lips before brushing them across her heart.

"You superstitious?" Mike asked.

"It doesn't hurt to ask for a little luck before doing something new or difficult." She closed her thumb and finger around the grip of the gun before wrapping her left hand around that to seal her grip.

Feeling a gentle pressure at the crown of her hair, Gina paused before lifting the weapon.

"For luck." Mike's gentle kiss and the husky tremor of his deep voice vibrated across her skin and eardrums, seeping inside her like the warmth of his body. Any trepidation she felt was under control, thanks to the support of this unexpected ally. "Let's do this."

She raised the weapon, tilting her head slightly to line up the sight and aim it at the paper target at the end of the firing lane. The gun dipped slightly when she moved her finger to the trigger guard, but she stabilized it with her left hand. The gun clicked when she pulled the trigger.

"Again," Mike instructed, sliding his hand beneath her elbow to steady her arm.

Gina aimed the empty weapon. *Click.*

"Again. Control it."

Click.

"Now use your left hand just to steady it, not

to keep your fingers on the grip." Her right hand shook as she made the adjustment. Mike's fingers stroked along her arm as he pulled away. "This one's all you."

Gina pressed her lips together, willing her grip to remain fixed as she took the whole weight of the weapon on her own. "Bang."

Steady. Her strength hadn't flagged.

"There you go." Mike praised her, setting the new clip of bullets on the counter. "Clear it and load it while I bring up a new target."

With Mike's hand at her shoulder to support the extra kickback of firing real ammo, Gina took aim at the target and fired off six shots. By the fourth bullet, she could feel the strain in her shoulder. By the sixth one, her hands were shaking.

"Easy," Mike warned, catching her right arm beneath the elbow to control the weapon as her hands slumped down to the counter.

But she kept hold of the gun, kept it pointed safely away from them. She batted his helpful fingers away to expel the magazine and clear the firing chamber herself before setting the gun aside. Gina exhaled an elated sigh as she pulled off her earphones. "I did it."

"That you did." Mike's hand settled at her hip, his long fingers slipping beneath her jacket, spanning her waist with a familiar ease while he nudged her to one side to secure the Glock.

Whether casually or with a purpose, he touched her often, as if he had the right to do so, and she wasn't complaining. "Have you considered using a lighter weapon?"

She shook her head as she removed her goggles and set them on the shelf beneath the counter. "I need one with stopping power." When she straightened, she asked, "So how did I do? I was six for six, center mass before I was injured."

Mike laughed as he pushed the button to bring the target up to the counter. "Give me a minute to check, Annie Oakley."

"I could learn to shoot left-handed if I have to."

But Mike pointed out the challenge in that solution. "How would you steady your grip and secure your aim? It's smarter for the strong to support the weak."

Was that supposed to be a metaphor? That he was strong and she was weak? Or that he believed she had the strength to overcome this setback? Mike was too nice a guy to give her a veiled put-down, so she chose to believe the latter.

Mike stowed his earphones, his body brushing against hers in the tight quarters of the booth. This was crazy, this distracted feeling she got whenever Mike was around. From the first moment she'd seen his long, powerful stride eating up the sidewalk on his afternoon run, there'd been something about him that pulled her attention away from the laser-sharp focus that had ruled most of her life. He was still a little too Dudley Do-Right compared to her streetwise bad girl persona for her to think they'd have any chance at making a relationship work—or even surviving a regular date. But she couldn't deny that he'd been a solid and dependable teammate since he'd taken over her recovery program. And for a woman who'd had very little *solid and dependable* in her life, Mike Cutler seemed an awful lot like that dream of peace and space and security she'd been chasing for so long.

She could count the individual holes in the target before it stopped in front of them, and some of her excitement waned. "I'm not six for six, anymore, am I?"

There was one hole right through the heart, the ultimate target for stopping a perp when cops fired their weapons. There were two more holes in the stomach area, two more in the left thigh and one completely off the map beneath the target's elbow. But the goal was to stop the assailant when threatened, not just to slow him down or give him a bellyache.

"At least they're all on the paper, and you didn't put a bullet in me or you." His humor eased some of her disappointment.

"You're right. Seven weeks ago, I couldn't even hold that gun." She tilted her gaze to Mike's clear blue eyes, his optimism feeding her own. "I am getting better. I just have to be patient."

"*Patient?* I didn't know that word was in your vocabulary."

"Ha. Ha. After all my hard work—*our* hard work—" she admitted, "I feel like celebrating."

"Celebrating?"

Gina reached up to stroke her fingertips along the chiseled line of his jaw, her hormones enjoying the perfect blend of ticklish stubble and warm skin. His eyes darkened to a deep cobalt at her touch. "Catnip." He shook his head slightly, his lips thinning into a smile. But before that smile fully formed, Gina's fingers were there, tracing the supple, masculine arc of his mouth. She heard a low-pitched rumble in his throat. Or maybe that visceral sound was coming from her. "Thank you."

She was stretching up on tiptoe as his mouth was coming down to meet hers. His lips closed over hers, and Gina slipped her left hand behind his neck, holding on as they dueled for control of the kiss. She delighted in the rasp of his beard against her softer skin as his mouth traveled leisurely across hers, pausing to nip at her bottom lip. When she mewed at the tingling stab of heat warming her blood, he grazed his tongue across the sensitive spot, soothing the sting of the gentle assault. But *leisurely* was frustrating, and *gentle* only made her hungry for something more.

When his tongue teased the curve of her mouth again, Gina parted her lips and thrust her tongue out to meet and dance with his. She slipped her right hand up around his neck as well, her sensitive thumb and finger learning the crisp edge of his short hair. When his fingers tunneled into her hair to press against her scalp and angle her mouth more fully against his, she didn't protest. When her hips hit the countertop and Mike's thighs trapped her there, she reveled in the feel of him surrounding her, consuming her. He tasted of rich coffee and man and desire, and Gina demanded the liberty to explore his mouth and learn his textures and delight in the chemistry firing between them.

"I like the way you celebrate," Mike growled against her lips before slipping his hands beneath her denim jacket to skim the length of her back and the curve of each hip through the cotton of her blouse. When his thumbs spanned her rib cage to catch beneath her breasts and tease the subtle swell there, she moaned in a mix of pleasure and frustration. What would it be like to feel his hands on her bare skin? To eliminate the barriers of clothing that kept her from touching him?

But even as she clutched at his shoulders, relishing the rare satisfaction of feeling warmth in every part of her body, from her taut, aching breasts to the tips of her toes, she knew this was a mistake. This kiss was moving too fast. Moving them in the wrong direction. Changing their relationship and jeopardizing every goal on her life list. "Mike…"

She made a token effort to push him away and ended up curling her fingers into the front of his polo shirt, latching on to the skin and muscle underneath.

"Tell me what *catnip* means." He reclaimed her mouth.

She helplessly answered his kiss.

"Hey, G. You in here?" A familiar voice shouted from the doorway, followed by the noise of heavy boots and other voices.

Gina shoved Mike back, abruptly ending the kiss. Even as his hands closed around her hips to steady her, she was twisting from his grasp.

"Gina?" Although he must hear the footsteps approaching, too, Mike's hoarse, throaty whisper demanded an explanation. Did he want an apology for cutting short that ill-advised make-out session? A reassurance that she had no regrets the kiss had happened? She wasn't sure what her honest answer would be. He tugged her jacket back into place and smoothed the wrinkles she'd made in the front of his shirt. "I get that the timing sucks, but we need to talk about this."

"What *this*? There is no *this*." With the walls of the booth granting them a few precious seconds of privacy, Gina wiped her copper lip gloss from his mouth, regretting the defined line her hasty withdrawal had put there. She swiped her knuckles across her own mouth, willing the nerve endings that were still firing with the magnetic need to reconnect with his lips to be still. "You're not my..." Boyfriend? Temptation? Best decision? He had to understand that she'd never meant her thank-you kiss to go that far. "I have to focus on me right now. On taking care of my family. I—"

He cut her off with a tilt of his head, warning her that they were no longer alone.

"There you are." Derek appeared around the corner of the booth. His gaze glanced off Mike and landed on her, his eyes narrowed as if he suspected something more than firing a gun had happened here. "Everything okay?"

"Of course," she answered a little too quickly. Although she could feel Mike's blue eyes drilling a hole through her, Derek seemed to buy it. She needed to change the subject before she admitted something she might never want to. "What are you doing here? Did you get things straightened out with your dad last week?"

"Yeah. He had another harebrained scheme to make easy money. I told him to stick with restoring the junk he finds in the scrapyard. I talked some sense into him. Sorry that he was being such a jerk." Grinning, he rattled on. "I heard you were down here, training with the captain's son. Brought you a surprise."

"A surprise?" she echoed.

Derek stepped aside to usher two other men, dressed in their distinct black SWAT uniforms, over to join them. "She's here, guys."

Mike moved out of the booth as a compactly built man with black hair joined them. Alex Taylor, one of her SWAT team trainers, grinned. "Hey, Galvan, we heard you were on the premises. Thought we'd stop in and say hi, see how you're doing."

As he stepped aside, another SWAT officer appeared. Despite the blond man's intimidating facade, she knew Trip Jones was a gentle giant until he went into SWAT mode. And then he was all serious business. His big hand swallowed up hers in a light grip as he smiled. "Look what the cat dragged in. Good to see you without the sling and hospital gown."

"Good to be seen. Thanks."

By the time she'd stepped out of the booth to join the minireunion, Alex was shaking hands with Mike. "Michael Cutler Jr. How'd you get involved with this fireball?"

"I'm her physical therapist." Apparently, Mike *did* know everybody at KCPD. Although the tension from that kiss and the guilt she felt at ending it so quickly still vibrated through her, making it difficult to think of what to say to these men she hoped to serve with one day, Mike didn't seem to have any problem joking with them as equals. "We're getting her back into fighting form."

"Don't do too good a job," Alex teased, including Gina in his smile. He swatted the big man beside him. "Trip's been practicing that takedown maneuver you used on him in training so you can't knock him over again."

Trip gave the teasing right back. "I stumbled over her. Didn't see her down there. Same problem I have when I'm sparring with you, Shrimp."

"You know I can take you out at the knees," Alex challenged.

Trip didn't bat an eye. "You know I can take you out, period."

Mike and Derek laughed, although both responses seemed forced to her. Mike wasn't in a laughing mood, and Derek was trying too hard to fit in as one of the team.

Gina inhaled a deep breath, determined to be a part of this camaraderie the men all seemed to share. "How do you all know Mike? Captain Cutler's summer barbecues?"

Trip splayed his hands at his waist, considering the answer. "Well, let's see. We first met when that creep had a bomb at Jillian's clinic. SWAT Team One was deployed, and Mikey here got up out of his wheelchair to get us inside to defuse the situation."

"Bomb?" Derek asked.

Gina looked up at Mike. "Wheelchair?"

She felt the sharp dismissal of Mike's blue eyes. He'd claimed she didn't know him, that he'd chosen to embrace his nice-guy persona *despite* his background, not because of it. What had confined him to a wheelchair and put him in the middle of a Bravo-Tango, or bomb threat?

Alex snapped his fingers. "No, wait. It was before that. We had to clear a building in No-Man's Land. Remember? There were a couple of druggies, and we were off the clock, but the captain called us in." Alex swatted Mike's arm. "You and Troy were outside in Captain Cutler's truck. Hey, how is Troy, anyway? The new business taking off for you two?"

"We could use a few more patients," Mike confessed, ignoring her silent questions. "As Gina pointed out to me—we didn't exactly set up shop in the most profitable part of the city. But we're making do. We'll turn the corner soon."

While they chatted, Derek stepped into the booth to pick up the discarded target paper on the floor. He let out a low whistle of appreciation. "Whoa, G. Is this your score? Looks like you're ready to come back to work."

"No. That's Mike's." Swallowing her pride in front of her peers, she pointed to the mutilated paper still hanging in the firing lane. "That guy's mine."

"Oh." Derek was at a loss for words. Alex covered the awkward moment with a cough.

Trip Jones, ever the practical one, stated the obvious. "You're going to have to do better than that to make SWAT."

Mike interrupted before she could acknowledge that she knew that score probably wouldn't qualify her to wear a sidearm for even regular duty. "Gina's improving every day. This is only her second time on the shooting range. Give it a couple more weeks and she'll be beating your scores."

"No doubt." Alex smiled, and Gina's spirits lifted a little. "This woman can do anything she puts her mind to."

Trip extended his hand to shake Mike's, bringing the brief reunion to an end. "You do good work, Mikey." He glanced down at Gina. "Heal fast," Trip said with an encouraging smile. "We need more good cops like you."

The door to the shooting range swung open at the same time as the radios clipped to Alex's and Trip's shoulders crackled to life.

"Taylor. Trip." SWAT Team Captain Michael Cutler strode across the room, the clip of authority in his tone and demeanor making Gina snap to attention. "Time to roll. We need to clear a neighborhood. Armed suspect at large."

"Yes, sir." Alex and Trip muted the same information coming over their radios, nodded their goodbyes and jogged from the room, heading toward the Precinct garage, where their SWAT van was located.

"You're the one I've been looking for, Johnson. Why aren't you at your desk?"

Derek pulled his shoulders back, too, at the direct address. "I was just heading up when I ran into Alex and Trip in the locker room."

"You're up to do a trainee ride on this call. You want to join us?"

"Definitely."

Gina's hand fisted with the same anticipation charging through Derek's posture.

"Gear up on the van. We're leaving as soon as I get there. This is an observation opportunity only," the captain reminded him. "You stay behind the front lines unless I tell you otherwise. Understood?"

"Yes, sir." Derek jogged off after the others, and the impulse to follow the action jolted through Gina's legs.

The older man backed toward the door. "Gina. Son."

Gina took half a step after him. "Any chance I'll get the opportunity to ride on a call with you again, sir? Keep my tactics skills fresh?"

Captain Cutler halted, his face lined with an apology. "I'm sorry, but you're a liability right now. Until you're declared fit for duty…"

"I understand." She nodded toward the door. "I'll let you go."

Mike's fingers curled around hers, down at her side between them. Holding her back from embarrassing herself? Or comforting her obvious disappointment over yet another reminder that right now she wasn't good enough? "What's up?" Mike asked.

The captain's pointed gaze landed on her, sending a silent message. "Somebody shot another cop. Frank McBride."

Gina's blood ran cold. First Colin Cho was shot. Then she and Derek were hit. And now this? With each incident, the injuries had grown more severe. "Is Frank...?"

"Ambulance is on the scene. No report yet."

"Go." The urgency of Mike's command matched her own sentiment. "Keep us posted. And be safe."

Captain Cutler's expression was grim as he hurried out behind his men.

Three assaults on police officers since the beginning of the year. Gina drew her hand away from Mike's, pacing several steps toward the door, needing to do something more than accept his comfort. She should be out there, protecting her brethren on the police force.

"Who's shooting cops?" she wondered out loud.

"I don't know," Mike answered. "But it sounds to me like KCPD is under attack."

Chapter Eight

"Could these incidents be related?" Mike speculated on the phone with his father. "They're all Kansas City cops."

His visit with Gina to the KCPD shooting range had stretched into the evening as they waited at headquarters for word on the injured officer. Once the news that Frank McBride had come out of surgery in fair condition, triggering a collective sigh around the Precinct offices, she'd agreed to let him drive her home. Troy would escort Frannie to her car and lock up the clinic, freeing Mike to stay with Gina. Now the city lights were coming on and streets were clogging with rush-hour traffic as the sun warmed into a glowing orange ball in the western sky. And though he hadn't followed his father's footsteps into the police force, Mike was just as eager as the woman sitting across from him in the cab of his truck to find out who the shooter might be and put a stop to these crimes against cops.

Gina leaned against the center console, following his half of the conversation. "Not just KCPD," she whispered. "The victims—Cho, Derek, McBride and me—we're all candidates for the new SWAT team."

Michael Sr. continued. "It sure feels personal to me. Every person hit since the beginning of the year has been one of the candidates we've been training for the new SWAT team. Maybe he's challenging himself to take down the best of the best."

"Gina was just mentioning that connection."

His dad's voice hushed. "She's with you now?"

Mike slowed for a stoplight. "I'm giving her a ride home."

"Good. I've put my team on alert and am in the process of notifying all the candidates to keep their guards up. Keep an eye on her for me, will you, son? This guy might just be toying with us, taking potshots at random cops. But I'm guessing there's something else at work here we don't understand yet. I'd like to think he can't bring himself to actually kill a cop. But more likely, he's working up his nerve and fine-tuning his MO. Once he's made one kill, he might decide he has a taste for it and come back to finish what he started."

The sunset warmed Gina's cheeks as Mike glanced across the seat at her. He didn't have to wonder at the twisting in his gut at the thought of the shooter making another attempt on her life. He had feelings for her. And her giving him the cold shoulder after that kiss wasn't making them go away. "Thanks for the update, Dad. Give Frank and Mrs. McBride my best."

Mike disconnected the call and placed the phone in the cup holder in the center console. "Dad noticed the same thing you did. The victims aren't just cops, they're all SWAT contenders."

She sat back in her seat with a deep sigh, giving him a rare glimpse of fatigue. "That has to be a coincidence. We're all uniformed officers. We haven't earned our SWAT caps and vests yet, so there's no way to distinguish us from anyone else at KCPD. How would this guy know?"

Mike shrugged as the light changed. He could think of several possibilities. "What about the car you've seen following you? Could be he's staked out the training center or Precinct headquarters. Maybe he's in the crowd when you go on observation calls with SWAT Team One and has seen you in action. Or he's hacked the KCPD computer system? There are a lot of ways he could get that information."

She grunted a sound that could have been a reluctant laugh. "You're not making me feel better."

"I'm not trying to. You're not the only one who wants to nail this guy and put a stop to the assaults on cops. It's personal to me, too."

Reaching across the center console, she patted

his arm, as if she thought *he* needed comforting. "Your dad is too high-profile of a police officer. A highly trained veteran, to boot. I'm sure the perp wouldn't go after him."

Unless a high-profile officer like his father *was* the ultimate target, and Gina, Derek and the others were a diversion to make KCPD think the attacker was hunting cops, in general, and not a specific target. Mike captured her hand against the warmth of his thigh. "I hate to think of some-one hurting you as simple target practice until he works up the nerve or the skill to make an actual kill shot."

Gina pulled her small, supple hand from his, as if even that small intimacy made her as un-comfortable as that kiss they'd shared. At least she wasn't discounting the attraction simmering between them, but she sure as hell didn't want to be feeling that way about him. Or maybe the aversion to the growing closeness was about something else. Bad luck with relationships. No interest in relationships. Or maybe the vulner-ability that naturally arose when two people cared for each other was the thing she wanted to avoid.

The petite beauty studiously ignoring Mike was turning out to be as complex a mystery as the recent spate of attacks they both wanted to solve.

She pointed out the next intersection where he

needed to turn and watched out the window as they entered the older neighborhood. The street narrowed and the houses got closer together and more run-down. The arching maple trees littered the small yards and sidewalks with their messy buds as leaves started to sprout. Gina shivered, and Mike discreetly turned on the truck's heater, although he suspected it was something mental, not physical, that had given her that chill.

Just as he thought they might reach her house in silence, Gina spoke again. "If the other incidents have all been a misdirection to throw the investigators off track, then who's his real target? Or if he just hates cops, why hasn't he killed any of us?"

"Thank God for that small favor."

"Seriously. Is it ineptitude? Is he toying with us?" Her shoulders lifted with a deep breath as she continued to speculate about the possibilities. "What if this has nothing to do with us being cops at all? What if it's something personal—that there's something besides a badge that connects all four victims? Or they're not connected at all? What if he's going after cops to make us think it's the uniform he's targeting and not a specific individual? How do we figure out who to warn? Who to protect?"

"Right now, we protect you."

"I can take care of myself."

"Right. While you're busy trying to find answers to these attacks, taking care of your family, vying to make the new SWAT team, and, oh, yeah—healing—you really think you have the capacity to watch your back, as well?"

She shook her head, stirring her dark hair around her face. "*Not* my bodyguard, Choir Boy."

Mike exhaled an irritated sigh. "That tough-chick shtick is getting pretty old."

"Look around you." She nodded toward the trio of young men hanging around a jacked-up car. "I have to be tough."

The young men, smoking cigarettes, all wore ball caps with the same telltale color underneath the brim, labeling them as gang members rather than a baseball team. Their souped-up car and air of conceit reminded Mike of his dangerous forays into No-Man's Land half a lifetime ago, when he'd sought out teens like that, instead of hanging with his true friends. He hoped it wouldn't take a tragedy like the ones he'd faced to convince them to make better choices and see the hope in their future. If Gina was the real target, and the other assaults were planned diversions, could the real threat be from someone close to home, like these guys?

"Gangbangers," Gina pointed out unnecessarily. She waved as they passed. Two of the boys waved back. One flipped them off.

Mike's hands fisted around the steering wheel as he remembered the faceless driver who'd pantomimed shooting Gina that morning outside the physical therapy clinic. "I assume they know you're a cop?"

"Uh-huh." He noticed her good hand fisting in her lap, too. "The one with the rude salute is in my sister's high-school class. My brother used to run with the other two. They're low-level members of the Westside Warriors, more bark than any real bite. I doubt they'll try anything unless their captain gives them the order to do so."

"Are they a threat to your brother or sister?"

"Not them." But someone else was? Gina's mouth twisted with a wry smile. "Can you see why I need that promotion at KCPD? It's so I can get my family out of this place."

Mike didn't have any platitude to offer. This *was* a dangerous part of the city. But it hurt to see that brave tilt of her chin and how all her responsibilities and the danger surrounding her day and night changed her posture. If he could make that smile a genuine one, for a moment, at least, he'd feel as though he was easing her burden. "And here I thought you just wanted a private bathtub."

Her dark eyes snapped to his before he heard the laughter bubbling up from her throat. "I'm a very serious woman with a very serious set of troubles. I don't have time for laughing with you."

Mike grinned. Fortunately, she'd said *with* him

and not *at* him. "That's officially part of my re-covery prescription for you. Laughing at least once a day."

She settled back into her seat and pointed out the window. "Turn here. It's the brick house with white trim and black shutters in the next block."

Mike spotted a row of three small houses whose owners seemed determined to maintain a clean, respectable appearance. The lawns were greening up, and there was a lack of junk or old cars sitting on the grass or at the curb. Gina's home was the one in the middle.

But the respite from worry and wariness was short-lived. "Did Captain Cutler say anything else about today's shooting?" she asked.

Mike nodded. "SWAT One did a building-to-building search in that block. Stopped traffic and checked vehicles. No sign of him."

"Any leads?"

Obliquely, Mike wondered if Gina had ever considered aiming for her detective's badge rather than SWAT. Although he suspected, with her position as the major breadwinner for her family, she didn't have a college degree yet, a prerequisite for becoming a detective. However, she was a natural at asking questions and ob-serving the world around her. "It was an ambush from an unidentified vehicle, just like with you and Derek. McBride was answering a call on a fight at a bar and grill downtown. Not far from

Precinct HQ. Still, the shooter was gone before backup got there."

"No description of the shooter or vehicle either, I bet."

"The only witnesses were a drunk still sobering up from last night and the bouncer. He was busy breaking up the fight. The two perps, of course."

When there was no empty spot to pull up in front of the house, Gina pointed him into the driveway. "Any bystanders hurt?"

Mike pulled his truck up to the garage door. "The only casualty was Officer McBride. Looks like the man in uniform was specifically targeted."

Unhooking her seat belt, Gina sat forward, facing him. "Wait a minute. Was the incident at the Sin City Bar and Grill?"

"Yeah. How'd you know?"

She pounded her fist on the console. "That's the bar where the bikers we chased away from the Bismarck house allegedly went before Derek and I were shot. I'd love to talk to the patrons there. See if the Bismarck brothers and their buddies were there today—maybe even part of that fight. They don't like cops. Maybe the whole fight was staged."

"How would they know Frank McBride would respond?"

"Maybe the guy was willing to shoot at any

cop who responded to the call. Or maybe he scouted the place out and knew that was Frank's beat." Her voice trailed away as she thought out loud. "Did he know the streets Derek and I patrolled? Or Colin Cho?" She was in full voice again as she turned to the door. "I need to see if anyone's followed up on this."

She tugged on the door handle and muttered a curse in Spanish when her recovering hand didn't cooperate quickly enough.

Mike caught her left wrist before she could reach across to open the door with both hands. "I know what you're thinking."

She tugged on his grip. "No, you don't."

Mike tightened his hold on her. "You aren't talking about making a phone call. You're planning on going to the bar yourself to investigate. Not tonight. You're home. You're staying put."

The tension left her arm and she smiled for a split second before forcing her right hand to fumble with the handle. "You're not the only means of transportation available to me. I can call a cab."

"The bar will either be closed or the cops investigating the shooting will have already talked to everyone."

"I'd be in the way. No help to anyone. Is that what you're saying?"

"What I'm saying is that it'd be a fool's mission right now. Plus, you need your rest and some dinner because I know you missed lunch."

"Not my nursemaid, Cutler."

"Not your chauffeur—yet here I am driving you. Not your friend—yet I'm the one thinking of your best interests. Not your lover." Her head snapped toward him, her startled eyes wide and dark as midnight. "And yet you kissed me like—"

She jerked her arm from his grasp. "Forget that kiss. I got carried away. I just wanted to thank you."

"A tough chick like you couldn't be interested in a nice guy like me, huh?" Why was he pushing this sore spot? Probably because his heart and ego had been battered one time too many. And a little of that rebel he used to be was getting tired of taking hit after hit. He reached across her, ignoring the clean, citrusy scent coming off her hair and skin, and pushed open the door. "Run if you want. You'll face down anything except what's happening between us."

Gina climbed out and circled around the hood of the pickup. But Mike was there to block her path.

She propped her hands at her hips and tilted her chin to face him. "Fine. Let's hash this out, Choir Boy. Is this where you tell me why you hung out in No-Man's Land as a teenager? Why you were in a wheelchair? Where you prove to me you're not so nice and that the two of us have enough in common to make something work after all?"

An image of his teenage friend Josh's mangled body flashed through Mike's thoughts, followed by the familiar upwelling of guilt he'd known since he was sixteen years old. The grief of his mother's death to cancer had sent him spiraling out of control, and the boozy haze of those wild months had cost him a football scholarship, the use of his legs and his best friend's life.

But the pricks of fear and grief and guilt were manageable now. He could acknowledge those feelings and lock them away before he did damage to anyone else's life. Or he allowed anyone else to be hurt when he could damn well do something about it. Including the stubborn Latina facing off against him. Gina needed to see him as her equal, as a partner who could help her if she'd only let him beneath that proud, protective armor of hers. "Let's just say I made some bad choices after my mother died. I found the solace I needed in No-Man's Land."

That took her aback. The sparks of defensive anger in her eyes sputtered out. "You did drugs? You had a dealer here?"

Alcohol had been his drug of choice. "I had *friends* willing to sell liquor to an underage drinker. I was happy to take them up on the offer.

Defied my dad's rules, trashed my chance at a football scholarship, got a friend killed."

Gina's gaze dropped to the middle of his chest as she reassessed her opinion of him. Was she trying to realign her image of Mr. Nice Guy Choir Boy with an out-of-control teen who lived with baggage from No-Man's Land the same way she did? Was the real Mike Cutler someone she could relate to and admire for getting his act together and making amends to the world for his mistakes every day of his life? Or did she now see him as the very kind of thing she was trying to get away from?

But Gina Galvan was nothing if not boldly direct. She tilted her gaze back to his. "How did your mother die? My mother had cancer."

All the no-one-can-hurt-me attitude had left her posture. Her voice warmed with compassion and understanding.

At the balm of that hushed, seductively accented tone, Mike wanted to reach out to her. He rested his hand on the hood of his truck, mere inches from where her fingers now rested. He stretched out his fingers, brushing the calloused tips against hers. When she feathered her fingers between his to hold on, something eased inside him. There were some understandings that crossed the barriers of backgrounds and economics and skin color. "Cancer. It was long and painful, and I didn't handle it well."

"Is that where you met Troy? Was he in a gang?"

"Nope. But that's where he got shot. In the wrong place at the wrong time during a drive-by shooting in the old neighborhood."

Her fingers danced against his palm, spinning tendrils of warmth, desire and healing into his blood with even that gentlest of connections. "How did you end up in a wheelchair? And why aren't you in one now?"

Gina's persistence would make her a fine detective. But Mike hadn't forgotten where this conversation had started. "If I answer all your questions, will you answer one of mine?"

She held his gaze expectantly, considering his request. Then she pulled her hand away and squared off her shoulders. Even without her flak vest, that woman's armor was locked down tight. "All right. What's your question?"

"Will you go to the Sin City bar on your own tonight after I leave?" She didn't need to say the word *yes*. He could read the guilty truth all over her face. Mike angled his gaze toward the orange glow of sunset on the horizon, shaking his head at the symbolism of his chances of making a relationship work with Gina going down right along with it. He'd better reel in his emotions like the champ here, and settle for finding answers and keeping her safe. "How about I pick you up in the morning and we go to Sin City together after your training session. Somebody should be there setting up by ten. And you won't be stepping on anybody's toes at KCPD then."

"Are you going to park outside my house tonight to make sure I stay put?" She'd barely uttered the flippant accusation before her expression changed. "Oh, my God, you are. You do know a truck this nice could get stripped in this neighborhood."

"I'm not leaving."

"Fine." Her cheeks flushed with irritation that he could be just as stubborn as she. "I promise to wait until you drive me in the morning if you promise to go home and not put yourself in danger because of me."

He couldn't make that deal. Mike planted his feet, tucking his hands into the pockets of his jeans and standing fast. If she was going into a dangerous situation, then he wasn't letting her do it alone.

"I'm going inside." She nudged his shoulder brushing past him, and Mike turned to follow her to the porch. "What are you doing?"

"Making sure you get inside safely."

"Nothing's going to happen to me between the curb and the front door."

He waited for the import of what she'd just said to sink in. A quick glance out to the street and he knew she was reliving the day she'd been shot. That short distance between the safety of her police cruiser and Vicki Bismarck's front door was exactly where she'd gotten hurt.

One look at the color leaving her cheeks and Mike turned her to the front door of her own home, sliding his fingers beneath the hem of her jacket and resting a supportive hand at the small of her back. He scanned up and down the block and through the neighboring yards, ensuring they were safe before nudging her forward. "Indulge a nice guy the manners his mama taught him, okay?"

Gina shivered at the polite touch but fell into step beside him as they climbed the single step onto the porch. "And here you are insisting over and over that you aren't so nice. Which Mike Cutler am I supposed to believe?"

"Both." Mike was grinning as they reached the door.

Gina pulled her keys from her pocket, but the door swung open before she could insert them into the lock.

A portly man with a strip of gray hair circling from his temples to the back of his head leaned heavily on his walker as he backed out of the doorway. "Gina, *la niña*. You are so late. We were getting worried." The elderly man raised his dark gaze to Mike. "You bring us a friend?"

"Tio Papi." Gina stepped inside to kiss the man's pudgy cheek while Mike waited in the doorway. A tiny woman with snow white hair

that curled like Gina's dark mane tottered up behind the man, drying her hands on a dish towel.
She gently chastised Gina's tardiness in Spanish
before the two women exchanged a hug. Keeping
her arm around the older woman's waist, Gina
made the introductions. "This is Mike Cutler. My
great-uncle, Rollo Molina. My great-aunt, Lupe."

Mike nodded a smile to each. "Ma'am. Sir."

"*The* Mike Cutler?" In addition to being over-
weight, Rollo Molina was a tad sallow-skinned.
The man must be struggling with circulation or
heart issues. But that didn't stop him from grinning from ear to ear and extending his beefy
hand. "I like to meet the man who saved my
girl's life. Now you see her every day. More than
we do. We worry, but not when she's with you."

Mike accepted the vigorous handshake. "She's
mentioned me, huh?" Why did that surprise him?
More importantly, why did knowing that she'd
talked about him with her family fill him with
a warmth and sense of connection that eased
the lingering sharpness of that argument they'd
had outside? Gina's dark eyes bored into his, as
if daring him to make something out of knowing she thought enough of him to tell her family about him. Oh, he was making something of
it, all right. He'd been recognized as "*The* Mike
Cutler," so she must have done more than simply mention his name. Mike winked at Gina. "I
imagine she's a hard one to keep track of."

Rollo laughed, pulling Mike into the entry-way and shutting the door behind him. "She has a mind of her own, *sí*?"

"Yes, she does."

Those dark eyes rolled heavenward. "Tio Papi…"

Gina started to explain something, but diminutive Lupe, a good three to four inches shorter than her great-niece, pushed past Gina to stand in front of Mike. She grabbed hold of his fore-arm, her body swaying slightly as she tilted her head back to study him through narrowed dark eyes. "You are Gina's friend? The young man who makes her well?" She tugged on the sleeve of Mike's jacket and he instinctively grasped her shoulders to steady her balance. "*¡Dios mio!* You are so tall. Your eyes are so *azul*, er, blue. Very handsome."

Mike glanced past her to Gina. *She* was the one blushing at her great-aunt's compliments. "Tia Mami… Mike was giving me a ride home. He can't stay."

"He doesn't eat dinner?" The fragile woman's grip on his arm tightened as if he'd imagined Lupe's balance issues. "I made chicken pozole soup. I put on a fresh pot of decaf coffee. And I have cheesecake empanadas for dessert. You like empanadas?"

"Yes, ma'am. But I don't want to intrude—"

"Come in, come in. You join us." A twenty-something man with a curling black ponytail strolled out of the kitchen, munching on an empanada. With her fingers latched on to the sleeve of Mike's jacket, Lupe pulled him past Gina and Rollo to swat the young man's arm. "Javi, those are for dessert."

"I'm hungry," he whined around the doughy sweetness in his mouth. "Who's the big dude?"

"This is Gina's friend, Mike."

He glanced up, then down at the white-haired woman. "*The* Mike Cutler?"

"My brother, Javier," Gina explained. "Where's Sylvie?"

"Yo, Mike."

Mike chuckled. "Yo."

Javier stuffed the last bite into his mouth and looked to his sister. "She's out."

Gina came up beside Mike, tension radiating from her posture. "Out as in running an errand? Or…out?"

Between Javier's darting glance at his great-aunt and Rollo's weary sigh as he shut the door, Mike could guess that, wherever Sylvie Galvan had gone, it didn't meet with the family's approval. Gina pulled out her cell phone. "Maybe I should go," Mike offered.

"Put that away." Lupe touched Gina's phone. "We have a guest. Sylvie makes her choices. She can eat without us." Then she shooed her great-nephew out of her path. "Go wash up. You need

good food before you go to work. Not sweets."
When she looped her arm through Mike's and
pulled him into the kitchen, he rethought his first
impression that she was a fragile grandmother.
Lupe Molina ran this home in a way that made
it easy to see why Gina was such a determined
woman.

"Tia Mami—"

"Senora Molina, really, you don't have to—"

"You saved my Gina's life." Lupe patted a
chair at one side of a rectangular white table.
"You sit. I feed."

Short of wrestling all one hundred pounds of
the elderly woman out of his way, Mike had no
choice but to do as she asked.

Once he took a seat as the honored guest, Lupe
bustled around the kitchen. By the time she'd set
an extra place setting and the fragrant, steaming food was on the table, Rollo, Javier and Gina
had joined them.

Mike enjoyed Gina's family as much as he enjoyed the spicy, hearty soup. Although his understanding of Spanish was limited to the classes
he'd taken back in high school, he had little trouble following the mix of English and Spanish and
the teasing, loving conversation. Lupe and Rollo
were animated and charming. Javier was interested in Mike's truck and Chiefs football. Gina
was quiet in the chair beside him and, though
Mike suspected that wasn't typical, at least she'd

stopped glaring a silent warning that he needed to leave as soon as possible.

If anything, she seemed to be assessing his response to her family and circumstances. He could understand her concern for her family's well-being. He could also understand her devotion to this tightly knit group. Maybe she was chalking up the apparent success of this dinner to him being a nice, polite guy, or maybe she was finally beginning to believe that he was more complex and able to relate to her and her background than she'd given him credit for.

Javier popped a third empanada into his mouth and took off for the bus stop a couple of blocks from the house to get to his job as an overnight custodian at a downtown office building. In between, Mike answered a barrage of questions: no, he wasn't married; yes, his father was the man Gina wanted to work for at KCPD; no, he didn't live with his dad and stepmom and brother; and, yes, he owned his own home off Blue Ridge Boulevard. Yes, he thought Gina was making a good recovery that would get her back on the police force, although he wouldn't promise how long it might take or if he could guarantee her a place on a new SWAT team.

They answered a few of his questions, too. He heard a bit about how Gina, Javier and Sylvie had come to live with their great-aunt and -uncle, and a lot about how proud they were of each of them. Gina had gladly taken on the job of supporting them, in addition to Rollo's pension check. Javi had enrolled in tech classes at one of the city's junior colleges. And Sylvie, who was as pretty as their late mother and prone to being late, was set to graduate from high school in just a couple of months.

Mike was sipping a cup of coffee that was richer and smoother than anything Frannie brewed at work and bemoaning the fact that he'd eaten that second empanada, when he heard the screech of tires braking on the street in front of the house.

He couldn't miss the instant bracing of alarm around the table, or the exchange of worried looks between Rollo and Lupe. Gina shoved her chair away from the table and hurried out of the kitchen.

"Gina," Rollo warned, reaching for his walker.

Mike stood, putting up a cautionary hand to keep the elderly couple in their seats. "I'll keep an eye on her."

The older couple reached for each other's hands across the corner of the table and muttered a prayer as he went after Gina. Not good.

He heard the slam of a car door and raised voices outside and saw Gina's curvy backside storming out the front door. Even worse.

"Gina?" Concern lengthened Mike's stride,

and he caught the storm door before it closed in his face.

Ignoring him, Gina stepped off the porch and marched down the walk toward a cream-colored luxury sedan parked catty-cornered across the end of the driveway. Outside the front passenger door of the slick, pricey car, a black-haired man was kissing a young woman with long, curling dark hair.

"Sylvie!" Gina called.

Sylvie? *That* was Gina's younger sister? The ankle boots and mini skirt showed so much leg that he'd question a grown woman wearing that outfit out of the house—much less a teenage girl.

Although the man who'd mimicked shooting Gina outside the clinic had driven a darker tan car, Mike found himself checking the license plate for a familiar 3-6. No match. Different car, different plate number—didn't mean Loverboy there wasn't a threat. And judging by the money invested in that car, he could afford more than one vehicle. "Gina, stop."

She didn't. Mike doubled his pace to catch up to her.

"I'll call you tomorrow," the would-be lothario murmured, looking over the girl's head to note their approach before adding an endearment in Spanish.

The teen pushed away from her adult boyfriend and hurried up the driveway. Although the sun had set and the street's tall maple trees blocked the moonlight, the glare of a nearby streetlamp cast a harsh glow across Sylvie Galvan's pretty face. The streaks of mascara running down her cheeks indicated she'd been crying.

The smudge of violet on her cheek bone hinted that she'd been hurt, too.

Gina noticed the mark, too, and caught her sister by the arms. She looked up into Sylvie's face, brushing the long hair away from the tears and the bruise. "Did he hit you?"

Sylvie sniffled. "I'm fine."

"Tell me what happened."

"Let it go, okay?" Then she tilted her gaze up to Mike. The young woman wiped her nose on a tissue and smiled, dismissing Gina's maternal concern and cop-like probing. "Who's this? You've been holding out on me. I thought you didn't have time for a man." She shrugged off Gina's grasp and circled around her older sister. "Wait. You've only talked about one guy lately— are you Mike Cutler? *The* Mike Cutler?"

"Guilty as charged." He took the hand Sylvie offered, noting the bruises on her wrist that were only slightly smaller than the span of his own fingers before turning her toward the yellowish streetlight to inspect the injury to her face. Although he kept his smile friendly, he was fuming inside. He'd seen marks like that on Frannie, courtesy of her ex, when she'd started working for him. "You hurt anywhere else?"

Sylvie tucked her hands inside the cuffs of her jacket, avoiding his questions, too. "You're cuter than Gina told us."

And Gina was angrier than Mike had ever seen her.

"Bobby Estes!" Gina whirled around and charged at the compact, muscular man in the black leather jacket. She spewed out a stream of Spanish Mike couldn't follow, but he could guess it had something to do with accusation and condemnation.

"Get inside the house," Mike ordered Sylvie before running after Gina. "Go."

When Sylvie started to protest, he glared her toward the front door, throwing out any essence of Mr. Nice Guy and replacing him with the stern taskmaster who wouldn't take no for an answer. With Gina's protective instincts raging like a mama bear protecting her cub, Mike had a sick feeling this confrontation was going to escalate into something a lot more serious than a lovers' quarrel.

The black-haired man leaned against his spotless car, laughing at Gina's approach. "You want a piece of me, Big Sister?"

That's when Mike spotted the telltale bulge beneath Bobby Estes's black leather jacket. Aw, hell. "Gun!"

Gina wisely backed off a step, her hand at her waist where her own weapon had once been. "I see it. Keep your hands where I can see them, Bobby."

While Bobby raised his hands into the air with a smug grin, the situation skipped from bad to worse and went straight to hell when a second man climbed out of the back of the car. He was armed, too. Mike shifted in front of Gina.

Gina shifted right back. "Hands on top of the car," she ordered. "Who's he?"

"A friend," Bobby answered. "I have a lot of friends. They protect me when I need it."

"Protect you from what?"

"People who threaten me?" With a gesture from Bobby, the second man held his position on the far side of the car, but did as she'd commanded, resting his hands on top of the car. "They're jealous of my success, or they want what I have."

Mike's stomach knotted right along with his fists at the obvious taunt.

But Gina kept her cool. "Like my sister? She's not a possession. If you really cared about her you'd leave her alone."

Bobby's arrogant amusement turned smarmy with a purse of his lips. "Maybe she's not the Galvan I want."

"You're using her to get to me?"

"Is it working?" he mocked, brushing his fingers against her hair.

This was a neighborhood power struggle, not a romantic foray. Still, it stuck in Mike's craw that the other man was putting his hands on her. He was already moving forward when Gina grabbed Bobby's wrist and flipped him against the car. "Stay away from Sylvie. Stay away from my family."

"See? Can't keep your hands off me." Bobby laughed. Mike turned his attention to the young man on the far side of the car, who looked more alarmed than amused by the wrestling match.

Gina bent Bobby's arm into the middle of his back, shoving him against the vehicle. That spike of jealousy instantly switched to concern that she would get hurt if this physical altercation escalated any further. "Get in your car and drive away," she warned, twisting his arm. "Lose Sylvie's number. Get out of our lives."

She pinched his wrist tightly enough for Bobby to curse in pain and, suddenly, the joke was over. "*My* neighborhood. *My* girl. Get your damn cop hands off me."

Bobby jerked his hips, knocking Gina back a step. Then he swung back with his free arm, the point of his elbow connecting squarely with her bad shoulder. Gina grunted with pain, grabbing her arm as she stumbled to the sidewalk.

Mike was right there to shove Bobby back

against the car, his forearm pressed against the bully's neck as he reached inside the leather jacket to pull the gun from Bobby's belt. "Leave. Now." With the smooth ease his father had taught him, Mike pointed the weapon over the roof of car at his buddy, who was reaching for his own gun. "Put it on the ground."

From the corner of his eye, he saw Gina scrambling to her feet and hurrying around the car to pick up the gun. Was she hurt? How badly? And just how much trouble would he get in if he pressed his arm more tightly against this sleaze-ball's windpipe?

Once Gina had the weapon trained on the other man and he'd wisely linked his hands over his head in surrender, Mike pulled back the Smith & Wesson pistol he was holding and leaned into Bobby's ruddy, angry face. "You got a license for this?"

"You a cop, white boy?" When Bobby shoved against him, Mike shoved right back.

The tendons in his back and legs strained as he kept the shorter man wedged in place. A zap of electricity shot down his leg as one of the old nerves pinched. Pain gave way to numbness in his right hip and thigh and would eventually set-tle into a dull, bruising ache if the injuries he'd lived with for more than a decade followed their usual pattern.

Mike gritted his teeth against any discomfort

and kept Bobby a prisoner while he watched Gina cover the second man. "You okay?" he asked.

"I'm fine," she ground out, grimacing with the strain of keeping the gun pointed at Bobby's friend. She needed both hands to keep the weapon from shaking, but there was no mistaking the authority in her tone. "Get back in the car. Get in!" The man didn't need a nod from Bobby to obey the order this time. Once he was in the backseat, with his hands out the window as she'd instructed, Gina lowered the weapon and circled around into the driveway again. "Let him go, Mike."

"You're sure?"

"Keep the gun, and let him go."

Bobby was laughing again as Mike released him and stepped beyond his reach. "You sure you can handle Officer Gina?" The neighborhood thug straightened his shirt and jacket as if this had been a civilized encounter. "I know how feisty Sylvie can be. All the Galvan women have fire in them."

"If you're so good at *handling* women, why did you need to hit a teenage girl?"

"Prove that I did." Bobby winked at Gina before circling around the hood and climbing behind the wheel of the car. He leaned toward the open passenger door. "May I have my weapon back, Officer?" When Gina hesitated, he added,

"If you arrest me, I'll file assault charges against your boyfriend here."

As far as Mike was concerned, anything he'd done to Estes was justified. Hitting a girl? Assaulting a police officer? But he wasn't the cop here, and he'd defer to however Gina wanted to play this. He was right beside her as she dumped the bullets from each gun into her palm and tossed the empty weapons back into the front seat before Mike closed the door.

"You'll be seeing me again, Gina," he promised before backing out into the street and speeding away.

The car veered around the corner and out of sight before Gina moved again. She stuffed the bullets into her jeans and turned back to the house. "I want to get these to the crime lab. See if they match the bullets from any of the police shootings. Bobby might have been targeting me and using the other incidents as decoys to throw the investigation off track."

Checking one last time to make sure Estes and his buddy stayed gone, Mike followed, wincing at the nerves still sparking through his hip and thigh. A hot shower or a long run would ease the kinks out of those muscles and tone down the minijolts. It had been a lot of years since he'd gotten mixed up in a physical confrontation that twisted his body like that, and he'd be paying for it later.

But he wasn't the only one in pain here. Although Gina was booking it up the driveway, he could hear the soft grunts with every other step and see her rubbing her shoulder.

"Are you all right?" he asked, catching up to her.

"Bruised my shoulder. My fingers are a little tingly. At least I'm feeling them, right? I'll be fine. I want to talk to Sylvie and find out what happened. If she presses charges, I'll serve the warrant on Bobby myself." She jumped onto the porch and reached for the storm door. "Could you drive me to the lab tonight? I don't want to have any issues with chain of custody—"

"Gina. Stop." Mike put a hand on her arm. "Take a breath. Everyone is safe."

"Are they?" Gina whirled around on him, and he spied something he'd never expected to see in her beautiful eyes. Fear. "I couldn't protect my family, Mike. I couldn't defend myself tonight. How the hell am I ever going to be a cop again?"

Chapter Nine

Mike closed the door to Lupe and Rollo's dimly lit room and moved down the hallway toward the bedroom Gina and Sylvie shared. It had been a long night at the Molina house. The family had gone through a second pot of decaf coffee, a phone call to Rollo's doctor, plus lots of tears, terse words and hugs. He peeked through the open doorway to see Sylvie perched on the corner of her daybed, dressed in black-and-gold sweats from her school, while Gina stood behind her, arranging her damp hair into a long braid.

As soon as her dark eyes made contact with his, Sylvie set down the ice pack she'd been holding against her swollen cheek and sprang to her feet. "How is Tio Papi?"

Leaning his shoulder against the doorjamb, Mike crossed his arms, hoping the relaxed stance would ease some of the worry and regret from her young face. "I checked his BP on the monitor again. He's resting comfortably now."

"But his pressure *was* elevated," she confirmed with a woeful sigh. "That's why he got dizzy."

Gina followed behind, winding a rubber band around the end of the braid. "His heart can't take much more of this kind of stress."

"I'm sorry, Gina. I never meant to upset him. Or Tia Mami," Sylvie apologized. "Is she okay?"

Mike nodded. Nothing that a little less worry and a good night's sleep couldn't fix for any eighty-year-old. "I encouraged her to lie down, too. She's getting ready for bed now."

"But she's upset?" Sylvie looked more little girl than woman without the heavy liner and mascara she'd worn earlier.

"Those bruises and guns would scare anyone." Gina hugged an arm around her sister's shoulders and guided her back to the bed. "Come on. You should rest, too."

"Do we need to call anyone?" Mike asked, knowing Gina had asked Sylvie some pointed personal questions about the nature of her assault while he'd helped their great-aunt and -uncle settle in for the night.

"We're good," Gina assured him, meaning there'd been no sexual assault. She cleared the ice pack and some first-aid supplies off the top of the purple comforter, while Sylvie stacked a rainbow of pillows against the wall. "I think the shower helped, but she hasn't shared many details yet."

Sylvie sat on the bed and reached for Gina's hand, pulling her to a seat beside her. Mike would have excused himself from the private conversation, but Sylvie's eyes filled with tears as she raised her gaze to his. "I love Bobby, but he... His friend Emanuel..."

Since she was including him in this conversation, Mike took a step into the room. "The other guy in the car?"

She nodded. "Emanuel said I was pretty and that he wanted to kiss me. Bobby said I had to let him." Gina's curse echoed the thought going through Mike's mind. "I didn't want to. But Emanuel grabbed me, and Bobby didn't try to stop him. Not at first. He laughed. I slapped Emanuel, and then Bobby..." She touched her cheek, and Mike's hands curled into fists. "He said I'd embarrassed him. That's when they got into an argument. Emanuel said the Lexus was his car, and if Bobby wanted to drive it then I had to... I was a bargaining chip," she sobbed. "I'm worth the price of a stupid car to him."

Gina wrapped her arms around Sylvie, rocking back and forth with her. "You can't see him again. You just can't."

How often had Bobby Estes promised Sylvie's affections in exchange for a fancy car? The image of a tan Mercedes circling around the PT clinic so that the driver could threaten Gina filled his thoughts. "Does Bobby borrow his friends' cars a lot?"

Although Gina shook her head, warning him away from asking questions related to *her* troubles, Sylvie answered, anyway. "Bobby has a different car about every week, I guess."

"Do you remember what he was driving two weeks ago?"

"Mike…" Gina chided. But the phone rang in her pocket, and she pulled away to check the number. "It's Derek calling me back. I need to take this." She wiped the tears from her sister's cheeks before standing and turning toward the door. Mike spotted the hint of moisture sparkling in her own eyes and started to reach for her. "No more questions," she mouthed before putting the phone to her ear and hurrying past him into the living room. "Hey, buddy, where were you? I called a couple of hours ago… Yeah, she's fine—or she will be. I need to ask a big favor…"

With a nod, Mike excused himself, too. "I'll let you get some sleep."

But the teenager popped to her feet. "Will you stay for a while?"

Mike supposed Sylvie didn't want to be alone until her sister returned. "Sure, kiddo."

She plucked a tissue from a box on the dresser and wiped away her tears. "I know Gina tries to be all badass. But I think Bobby scares her. I know he scares Rollo and Lupe. But things are a little calmer with you here."

"He scares her because you got hurt and she couldn't stop it. Doesn't mean she's going to back down from any of his threats. Your sister's a brave woman."

"I know." She rolled her dark eyes. "And I know I'm...a headache for her. But we're all trying to find our own way out of this part of town."

"Bobby isn't your way out."

Sylvie shredded the tissue in her fingers before tossing it into the trash. "Maybe not. But I thought he cared about me. Until tonight. And there aren't many guys like you around here."

"White guys?"

She smiled at his teasing chuckle. "Nice guys." Maybe that was a compliment, after all, because she padded across the rug and wrapped her arms around Mike's waist, squeezing him in a hug. "Don't let Gina scare you off. She really likes you, you know."

He knew. But did Gina? And given the career and family priorities she pursued to the exclusion of anything personal, would it make any difference if she did?

He pressed a chaste kiss to the crown of Sylvie's head. "You're going to be okay."

"I know."

"I'll be out on the couch tonight. Don't worry

about Bobby or your aunt and uncle or Gina. Sleep tight."

He patted her shoulder before she moved away and crawled onto the daybed, leaning back against the pillows. After pulling a fuzzy blanket over her lap, she grabbed her phone, plugged in her ear buds, turned on her music and tuned him out the way a normal teenager would.

Mike grinned as he pulled the door shut, liking this version of Sylvie Galvan a lot better than the frightened young woman who fancied herself in love with Bobby Estes.

He found Gina in the darkened living room, sticking her cell phone into the pocket of her jeans. She flipped on a lamp beside the sofa where Lupe had set out a pillow and a blanket. He recognized the tight set of her full, bow-shaped lips as she waged an internal battle between the urge to tell him to leave and the desire to give her family the reassurance his presence here seemed to provide. Although hushed, so as not to disturb anyone else in the house, her tone was strictly business. "Derek said he'll do the paperwork for the lab and file a report on the assault."

Mike whispered back. "The one on you? Or the one on your sister?"

"Both."

"Good."

Gina nodded as she circled around the couch

and gestured for him to follow her toward the front door. "Thank you for staying so long, but it's late. You have work in the morning and need to get some sleep. I've checked the doors and windows twice already. Sylvie's not sneaking out, and I'm not letting anybody get in. We'll be all right."

"I know you've got your bases covered. I'm staying, anyway."

She tilted her proud chin to his. "Because I'm weak?"

"You're the strongest woman I know." He reached out to brush his knuckles across her soft cheek, not liking the chill he felt there. "I don't want anything to happen to this family. Another set of eyes and ears can't hurt. If I can help—"

"You have helped. You always help." She tipped her cheek into his hand, and the silky curls of her hair tickled his skin, waking the nerve endings that flared to life whenever she got close. "Sometimes I wonder if you're for real. You're just too damn—"

"Don't you dare say *nice* again, like it's some kind of plague." Gina's pupils dilated in the shadows, turning her eyes into rich pools of midnight. She fisted her hand in the front of his shirt, and Mike knew he was in for another argument as she tugged him toward the privacy of the kitchen. "What now? I swear, woman…"

Once his shoes reached the tile floor, she

yanked harder, untucking the front of his shirt and pulling him off balance as she bumped into the lower cabinets. Mike braced his hands against the countertop on either side of her so he wouldn't crash into her. But before he could ask what this sudden escape from the living room was all about, she slipped her damaged hand behind his neck and pulled his mouth down to hers.

The unexpected contact shot a bolt of lightning through him, igniting an urgent heat. There was something purposeful, maybe a little angry, in the way she clung to him and fused her mouth to his. Where that anger was directed, Mike couldn't tell. And, at the moment, Mike didn't care. Instinctively, his mouth moved over Gina's, claiming what she offered. Her lips softened, parted. With a husky gasp that went straight to his groin, Gina swept her tongue between his lips. Her fingers clutched at the edge of his jaw, stroking across his beard stubble, holding their mouths together. This wasn't anger; this was need. This was attraction simmering out of control. This was the inevitable release of every emotion roiling through this house tonight.

Mike understood that fire. That desperation. That crazy need to connect to the one person who could ease the fear, the anger, the need and the passion that had grown too powerful to control anymore.

Slipping his hands to her waist and pulling

her body into his, Mike took control of the kiss, suckling on her sweet bottom lip, soothing the trembling response with his tongue. She pulled at the hem of his polo until she could slip her hands inside to palm the skin of his chest and stomach, branding him with her desire. He returned the favor, tugging her blouse from her jeans and splaying his fingers over the smooth curve of her back.

He felt the chill of her skin as he explored the length of her spine and flare of her hips. He dropped gentle kisses against her eyebrows and cheeks and the rapid beat of her pulse beneath her ear. The woman was responsive in a way that made him feel powerful, male, whole. Gina warmed at every spot he touched and cooed soft, excited moans that hummed in her throat. Her fingers raked through his hair, roamed over his shoulders, traveled inside his shirt, kindling an incendiary response that made him want to reclaim her lips and loosen the snap of her jeans and tug down the zipper so he could dip his fingers beneath the elastic band of her panties and fill his hands with that irresistible backside.

"Is Sylvie okay?" she murmured against his mouth, running her fingers along the column of his throat, nipping at the point of his chin, turning his response into a hoarse growl.

"You want to talk *now*?"

"Yes." She tipped her head back as he trailed

his lips down the arch of her throat, seeking out the source of those sexy hums. She whimpered when he found a particularly sensitive bundle of nerves. "No. Is she?"

Mike chuckled his response against her skin. "She'll be fine. The bruises on her cheek and wrist are superficial. It might not hurt to talk to a counselor, though."

"I'll arrange it." Gina stretched up on tiptoe, her small breasts pillowing against his chest as she guided his mouth back to hers for another hungry kiss.

Mike indulged himself in the pleasure firing throughout his body. He grabbed her sweet, round bottom and lifted her, thinking he was never going to get enough of this woman until he was buried deep inside her. His hard length pushed against the zipper of his jeans, seeking out the heat of her body.

This make-out session was going from zero to sixty in a matter of seconds. And while their bodies were definitely willing, Mike had to wonder if their brains were on board with where this was headed. He moved his hands up to feather his fingers into her hair and rested his forehead against Gina's, sucking in a deep breath of much-needed air. "I need to understand the rules here. There is no *this*, no *us,* yet it's all right for you to kiss me like I'm the only snack on a deserted island?"

"Forget the rules. Just…" She tipped her head to seal their lips together in brief kiss. "I don't like being scared or vulnerable."

"Tell me about it." He welcomed the cinch of her arms around his waist, as he took her mouth in a leisurely kiss. "Sounds like you've talked to your family about me. Maybe said a couple of nice things."

"Don't let it go to your head, Choir Boy."

Oh, but there were a lot of other things going straight to his head.

Her hands slipped beneath his shirt, singeing the skin on his back. "I don't like feeling as if I can't handle myself in a fight."

"You'll get there. I promise."

The kiss jockeyed back and forth with forays and acceptance, with tantalizing discovery and revisiting a favorite angle or caress. "I'm glad you were here, that you had my back."

"Anytime."

"No. Not any—" she gasped as his palm settled over her breast, squeezing the proud nipple between his thumb and palm through the lace of her bra. She buried her face against his chest, pushing the pert handful into his greedy hand, her soft gasps belying her breathless words. "I want this, but… I can't do a relationship. I don't have time. It wouldn't be fair to you…all my responsibilities—"

"Do you hear me complaining?" He squeezed

her bottom and lifted her again. She wrapped her legs around his waist, and Mike's pulse thundered in his ears. He wanted her. She wanted him. "There's just now." He spun around, leaning against the sink. But her knees butted against the countertop. "We're both adults. We're safe." He spotted the chair sticking out from the table and carried her toward it. "Don't overthink this."

He sank onto the seat, pulling Gina into his lap. He couldn't help but push against her as her thighs squeezed around his hips. They kissed as their hands fumbled between them. Mike spread his thighs to ease the tightness in his jeans. But he'd miscalculated his position on the chair, and his right leg slipped off the seat. Gina shifted. Mike caught her, planting his foot to keep her in place. He moaned against her mouth, a blend of anticipation and frustration as the inevitable jolt of electricity sparked down his leg.

Hugging her tight to his body, Mike winced as he stood to alleviate the pressure on the pinched nerve. His broken body was betraying him. Just when Gina was letting him get close. Ah, hell. Now the leg had gone numb.

"Mike? Put me down." Gina scrambled out of his grasp, pushing away but clinging to his arms until she found her balance. No, she was steadying him. "Are you hurt? Do you need to sit down?"

"Standing is better." He pulled Gina back into

his chest, dropping his chin to the crown of her hair. "I'm sorry. Nothing like a twinge of the old bursitis and my leg going numb to put a damper on things. Just let me hold you for a second, okay?"

But the woman couldn't keep still. Now he'd just added himself to the long list of things she had to worry about. "What happened? Did Bobby hurt you?"

"Be still for a sec. I'll be fine. It's an old war wound acting up."

"Huh?"

When she stilled and leaned into him, Mike pulled her arms back around his waist and breathed deeply against her dark, fragrant hair, willing the numbness and the lingering desire still firing through his system to abate. "I was in a car wreck when I was sixteen. A friend was driving me home because I was too drunk to be responsible for myself. He died. Helping me. Pretty much every bone below my waist was shattered. Tore up muscles and nerves. The doctors weren't sure I was going to walk again."

Her arms tightened around him. He felt both hands hooking into the back of his belt as she nestled her cheek against his heart. "Your friend died?"

"Leave it to you to pick up on the important detail." Mike distracted himself from the guilt and regret by sifting her hair through his fin-

gers. Although this stance gave him a bird's-
eye view of that sexy bottom he wanted to grab
again, he ignored the impulse and savored her
willingness to simply be close to him without
any kind of protest. "There's some residual nerve
damage I deal with. Regular exercise keeps the
weight off the joints and the muscles strong, but
sometimes I'll twist wrong or even sleep wrong
and tweak a nerve. Or the weather changes and
all the metal pins and wires inside let me know
it. But I'm walking now, with no braces and
no cane. I can make love to a beautiful woman
again—on most nights." His wry comment only
made her snuggle tighter. "I can run again. So
I'm not complaining. Sorry to start something I
couldn't finish."

She shook her head. "*I* started it. And I'm not
complaining. I'm just glad you're here."

"Me, too."

"We're a pair, aren't we? Gimpy and Ho-
palong. Maybe between us there's a whole person
who can take down the bad guys." She released
his belt to rub her hands over the backside of
his jeans. Whether consciously or unconsciously
done, the tender strokes across the muscles at the
small of his back and hips felt good. The physical tension in him eased and the air around them
cooled, even as something warmer and more pro-
found than the desire they shared took hold in-

side him. "I'm sorry for all of the trouble I've brought to your life."

"Trust me, Tiger. I know trouble. You ain't it." He leaned back against her arms, framing her face between his hands and tilting those rich brown eyes up to his. He dipped his head to press a firm kiss to her beautiful lips before reluctantly pulling away. "You need to go to bed. Alone." He pulled her hands from his hips and backed away before he couldn't leave her. "Do not sneak out of this house and go to that bar by yourself. Do not take on Bobby Estes by yourself. Take care of your family tonight. Rest. I'll be here in the morning when you wake up."

"You can't stay." Despite her words, she pawed at him, buttoning his shirt, smoothing down the spikes of his hair. If she kept touching him, they were going to end up right back where they'd been a few minutes ago. "You shouldn't."

Mike listened to what she needed, not what she wanted. He stopped her hands from their busywork and squeezed them in his grip. "This is moving too fast, and you're not comfortable with that. I get it. I don't want you to regret anything that happens between us."

She nodded. "I don't want you to regret anything, either. I'm kind of a mess tonight."

"Join the crowd. The timing sucks. That's all." He released her hands and brushed a thick curl off her cheek, tucking it behind her ear. "Mind if

I call a couple of friends at KCPD and ask them to make a few extra passes through your neighborhood tonight?"

This time, she pulled his hand away. But she was smiling. "I'd appreciate it."

"Consider it done." He leaned in for one more peck on the lips, thought better of it considering his willpower around Gina and turned her toward her bedroom. "I'd better go to that couch now, or I never will."

He followed her into the living room, pausing at the couch as she quietly opened the bedroom door and peeked in. Even through the shadows cast by the lone lamp, he could see her smiling.

"Sylvie asleep?" he whispered.

Gina nodded before opening the door wider. Mike glanced down at his wrinkled shirt, grinning at the mismatched buttons and buttonhole Gina had missed in her haste to redress him.

"Mike?"

He glanced up to see her padding back across the hall to meet him. "Something wrong?"

She drew her shoulders back, steeling her posture before speaking. "It's the five o'clock shadow. The way it's just enough beard to be interesting, but not so shaggy that it obscures your face." He frowned in confusion. She touched his face, running her fingertips along the line of his jaw. "Catnip," she explained. "That's my catnip. What I find attractive on a man. Something about the angles and the rawness is *muy masculino*. There's something a little bad boy about it that I want to touch."

He didn't need to be fluent in Spanish to understand that compliment. His face eased into a smile beneath her touch. He turned to kiss her palm before she pulled away. "Happy to oblige. Now get some sleep. I'll stay up and keep an eye on things until the first black-and-white drives by. See you in the morning."

Mike waited for the bedroom door to close behind her before he went back into the kitchen to splash some cold water on his face, tempering those last vestiges of desire lingering from that kiss. He called a couple of friends from his father's SWAT team and explained the situation, needlessly promising a free lunch or workout at the clinic in exchange for their help watching the house.

Once his friends Trip and Alex had arrived and parked their truck across the street from Gina's, Mike peeled off his shirt, belt and shoes and stretched out on the couch that was too short for him. It was after midnight when he heard the hushed sound of a door opening and closing. More curious than alarmed, he peeked around the end of the couch to see Gina in a long-sleeved T-shirt and pajama pants. Instead of heading for the bathroom, as both Lupe and Rollo had done earlier, she kissed her knuckles and rubbed them against her heart.

Mike remembered the superstitious action from the shooting range. "What do you need luck for at this time of night?"

She didn't startle at his teasing voice from the shadows. "Not luck. Courage."

He sat up, concerned by her answer. "Gina?"

"I saw the men out front. Thank you." She circled the sofa and sat beside him. "I don't want to have sex. I'm not ready to complicate us like that yet. But…could we snuggle for a little bit? I can't seem to get warm again, and I can't sleep when I'm cold, and…"

Relieved to know that Sylvie and everyone else in the house were safe, he wrapped the blanket around her and pulled her into his arms. "You don't have to be the strong one all the time. Take a breather tonight. I've got you."

Turning onto his side, he stretched out on the couch behind her, spooning his chest against her back. "This doesn't mean anything," she insisted. "I'm just cold."

"Understood." Grinning at the tough act he wasn't buying, Mike draped his arm around her waist and tucked her as close as the blanket and dimensions of the couch allowed. "Warm enough?"

She nodded, resting her head on his arm. "This doesn't make your legs cramp or hurt, does it?"

"Nope. Your shoulder okay?"

"It doesn't hurt at all when I lie on this side." Several seconds passed before he felt her body relax against his. "Sylvie gets up at seven for school."

He ignored the bottom nestling against his groin and reached for his phone. "I'll set my alarm for six."

"You're driving me to the crime lab and Sin City Bar in the morning."

"Yes, ma'am."

"Could we do that before my therapy session?"

Mike's laugh was as hushed as the shadows surrounding them. "Only if you stop talking and get some rest."

"*Not* my mother, Choir Boy." Her answering laugh faded into a yawn.

He nudged aside the dark curls at the nape of her neck and pressed a kiss there. "How about your partner?"

She brushed her lips across the swell of his bicep. "Deal. For now."

The strong fingers of her right hand latched onto his. In a matter of minutes, the tension eased from her body, and her soft, even breath against his skin let him know that she'd finally fallen asleep. "I'll be your armor tonight, Tiger," he whispered.

Mike settled into the most comfortable position he could manage and drifted toward sleep himself, knowing three things. One, Gina liked to keep things even between them—he'd revealed a secret, so she had, too. Two, there was far more danger surrounding this woman than even he'd realized. And three, the attraction simmering in his veins, the unexpected caring that took them beyond therapist and patient, or even friends, was mutual, no matter how stubbornly independent she tried to be.

Logically, he could see the pattern of his life repeating itself: play Knight in Shining Armor to a woman who needed him. Stir up his hormones and get his heart involved. The next inevitable step would be her realizing she no longer had a use for the strength and support he provided, and him getting hurt again.

But he couldn't stay away from Gina. Out of all his relationships—Caroline, Frannie, others who'd grown tired of Mr. Nice Guy before anything real had started—none of them had gotten him twisted up inside as fast and feverishly as Officer Gina Galvan. Her bravery and vulnerability, her fierce determination to improve her standing and protect her family, her passionate impulses and the stubborn emotional shield she couldn't quite keep in place—all got under his skin and inside his head and into his heart, refusing to answer to caution or logic.

He was falling for Gina Galvan. Falling hard and fast. And the closer he got, the more he realized there were too many ways he could lose her.

Chapter Ten

Gina fingered the badge clipped to the belt of her jeans, trying not to feel as if she was impersonating an officer this morning, as she stared out the window of Mike's pickup at the heavy steel door below the Sin City Bar sign. Technically, although she was on medical leave, she was still a member of KCPD, and she'd earned the right to wear this badge. And, until that losing skirmish with Bobby Estes last night, she'd believed she was always going to be a working cop again. An elite cop. A SWAT cop.

Now she was feeling a bit like Sin City's fraudulent facade. At night, their sign lit up with red and yellow bulbs, bathing the entryway in a warm color, welcoming patrons. But the bright sunlight of a chilly spring morning revealed chipped white paint on the outside walls. Rust at each corner of their sign stained the painted brick and faded awning over the door. With the blinds drawn at every window, there was no promise of a party at a friendly bar to draw in customers.

Just like wearing the badge didn't mean she could do this job the way she wanted to again.

Looking at the row of motorcycles and the beat-up van in the parking lot beside the bar, she was certain she was about to get another opportunity to chat with Gordy and Denny Bismarck and their biker buddies. And she suspected them being here at this time of day meant they were either very good friends with the manager and bartenders she'd hoped would break their alibi— which meant that probably wasn't going to happen—or they had gotten wind of KCPD looking into them as the potential cop shooters and they were here to make sure that no one gave them up. Either way, she was on their turf. Asking questions and getting straight answers wouldn't be easy, even on her best day.

"You ready to go play good cop/bad cop?" Mike's angular features crooked into a teasing smile as he pulled in beside the van and turned off the engine.

Drawn from the doom and gloom of her thoughts, Gina smiled back. One more day and that sexy beard stubble of his would cross the line into scruffy.

But in the dark hours of last night, she'd admitted there were plenty of other reasons why Mike Cutler was her catnip. Her family had felt reassured by his presence at the house, and anyone who was that kind and patient with her family was a hero in her book. That long, hard, rebuilt body had been a furnace at her back, keeping her warm and secure enough to enjoy the best night's sleep she'd had since the shooting. His hands had awakened an answering need inside her with each purposeful touch. And she shouldn't even think about the gentle seduction and commanding firmness of his mouth moving over hers. Even his do-the-right-thing stubbornness that matched her own was becoming less of a frustration and more of a type of strength she respected. She'd lowered her guard with Mike last night, both physically and emotionally. She'd felt normal, free of all her burdens, for a few hours. Mike Cutler managed to be strong for her without making her feel weak or foolish or at any kind of disadvantage.

She'd never expected that a man could make her feel like that—like she could fall in love with him if she wasn't careful.

She reached over the console to brush her fingers across his jaw. *Sí.* She had definitely developed a craving for that handsome face. "Not a cop, Choir Boy."

The color of his eyes darkened like cobalt at her touch. Just like that, with a piercing look and the ticklish caress of his beard beneath her sensitive fingertips, her stomach tightened with desire.

But she was here to work. She hadn't been lying when she'd said she couldn't fit a relationship into her life right now. If she could, there would be only one candidate. But reality made falling in love low on her priority list. It made falling in love with Mike nearly impossible. She pulled her fingers away and unbuckled her seat belt. She eyed the officer stowing the last of the yellow crime scene tape from Frank McBride's shooting into the trunk of the black-and-white police cruiser already in the parking lot.

"Looks like Derek's ready for us." Having her partner here made this interview sanctioned, despite her own self-doubts. He'd met them at the crime lab earlier so she could deliver the bullets she'd taken from Bobby's and Emanuel's guns to the ballistics tech. He would run a comparison between them and the spent rounds recovered from the police shootings, including her own. "You wait in the truck."

Mike shook his head, pocketing his keys in his jacket. "I can't very well watch your back from here."

Gina paused with her hand on the door handle. "Derek will have my back. I'm guessing the Bismarck boys aren't going to cooperate, and I need you to stay safe."

"How about we double our efforts?" He pointed through the windshield to the garage on the opposite side of the bar's parking lot. "An auto-

repair and customization shop right next door
to their hangout? Want to bet that one or more
of them works there? I can wander in and ask if
anyone there remembers them from the day of
your shooting, or if they saw them here yesterday
when Frank was shot. Maybe I'll get an estimate
on rotating my tires."

"And, while you're in there, see if you spot
any familiar vehicles like the rusty old SUV the
shooter used or the tan Mercedes that's been following me?"

"Is that a bad idea?"

"No. It's a smart one." Derek was out of the
cruiser, heading toward the truck. As uneasy as
the thought of Mike investigating on his own
made her, she couldn't deny that he had inherited all the right instincts about being a cop from
his father. Other than the fact he was unarmed.
But then, so was she. "All right. You check out
next door while Derek and I see if we can break
anybody's alibi. But if the Bismarcks or their
friends *are* there, I don't want you to engage any
of them. Turn around and get out of there. I'll
meet you back here."

"Ten minutes give you enough time?"

Gina nodded. "No heroics, okay? Just get information."

"Yes, ma'am."

Derek was waiting beside the truck when she
shut the door. He rested an arm on the butt of the

gun holstered at his waist, his eyebrows arched in confusion as Mike jogged across the parking lot and entered the automotive shop. "I thought Cutler was just driving you around until you're cleared to do it yourself. What's he up to?"

"Detective work." Kissing the back of her fingers and rubbing them against her heart, she sent up a silent prayer that Mike wasn't on a mission that could get him hurt. Then she butted her elbow against Derek's and headed for Sin City's front door. "Come on. We'd better do the same."

On a different day, if she was in uniform and back on patrol, Gina would have run in the bar's owner, Vince Goring. The myopic manager was already serving a drink to a dazed old man who, judging by his ratty appearance and eye-watering stench, had probably been sitting on the same barstool since closing time the night before. She wondered if he was the drunk who'd allegedly witnessed Frank McBride's shooting yesterday afternoon.

Nothing about this quest for answers was going smoothly. The deep voices and laughing conversation from the back of the bar fell silent by the time her eyes had adjusted to the dim lighting. She'd been hoping she could talk to the owner alone, find out who'd been tending bar that wintry afternoon when she'd gotten shot. But Vince was carrying a tray of coffee mugs to the back booth, where Gordon and Denny Bismarck, Al, Prison Tat Guy and one of their pot-bellied buddies were sitting. Denny pulled his flask from his pocket and doctored his coffee before passing the container around the table. Oddly enough, none of them seemed to be sporting a black eye or broken nose, or other signs that'd they'd been involved in the fight that had lured Frank McBride here. But in this dim lighting, it was hard to tell.

Still, she wasn't here about serving drinks to someone who'd already had too much, or citing a barkeep who allowed patrons to bring in their own alcohol. Letting the glare from Denny Bismarck's dark eyes fuel her resolve to conduct this interview, she ignored him and the whispered conversations at the table, while Vince shuffled back to the bar where she and Derek stood.

"Mr. Goring." Gina made no effort to whisper. If Bismarck and company knew she was here, then they had to suspect she was asking questions about them. "That group of men at the back table—are they regulars?"

Vince pushed his thick glasses up onto the bridge of his nose before answering. "Sure. Al and Jim work next door at the body shop."

Gina had done her homework. She pointed to her neck. "Jim Carlson is the guy with the tats?" She remembered Al Renken, the van driver. He was bald.

"Yep. You friends with them?"

The last man, Aldo Pitsaeli, was the guy who'd been worried that day about getting in trouble with his wife. Denny and the others had been with Gordy at the Bismarck house before the shooting. Did the five men always travel in a pack? Would they alibi any member of their group who wasn't there? Even if he left to go shoot a couple of cops? "We're acquainted."

That seemed good enough for the barkeep to start talking. "Gordy got his bike customized at the shop. Denny, too. Although they sometimes drive a '75 Bronco SUV they inherited from their daddy. If you ask me, they ought to take that wreck to the scrap-metal yard, or else get *it* customized. All painted up with a couple new fenders, folks might go for it."

She wasn't here for a lesson in auto mechanics, either. "They come in here a lot?"

He picked up a rag to wipe down the bar around the drunk who never moved. In fact, she could hear him snoring. "They hang out with Al and Jim when they're workin'. Sometimes do odd jobs over there. They're all motor heads. They come over here a lot when Al or Jim go on break or have a day off."

Derek tapped her on the arm and straightened behind her. But Gina was already aware of Denny Bismarck standing up and his younger brother sliding out of the booth behind him. She doubted they'd do anything stupid like attack a uniformed officer so soon after yesterday's shooting, but she still felt the urgency to ask her questions faster. "Do they ever come into the bar in the afternoon?"

"I guess." He snapped his fingers. "Oh, you mean like those cops were asking yesterday?"

"I'm more interested in seven weeks ago, January twenty-sixth," she clarified. "Were you working the bar that day? Were they all here?"

Vince nodded. Then frowned and shook his head.

Gina's hand curled into a fist. "Yes or no? Were they here that afternoon?"

"Seven weeks is a long time to remember something."

As far as Gina was concerned, seven decades wouldn't be long enough for her to forget that day. "Well, can you remember yesterday? There was a fight in your bar. A black police officer responded. He was shot out front."

"Oh, yeah. That was real bad. I didn't know what was going on until I heard the shots. Thought it was an engine backfiring next door."

"Who was in the fight?" She pointed to the back of the bar. "Was it any of those guys?"

"G?" Derek's hand brushed the small of her back, alerting her to the group of men ambling their way.

Gina caught and held Denny's glare as she asked Vince a follow-up question. "Are they al-

ways here together? The brothers, their friends—
in a group like this morning?"

"I guess."

"Was one of them missing?"

"Yesterday?" He looked at the group of approaching men, as if seeing their faces for the
first time. "As I recall, they were out front by
the time I got there. Fight was over. The officer
was writin' folks up. Maybe they were in the bar.
Guess they could have come out of the shop."

Gina bit down on her frustration and kept a
friendly smile on her face. "All of them? What
about seven weeks ago?"

Vince adjusted his glasses again. "Come to
think of it, Gordy wasn't here that day."

No. He'd been sitting in the back of her police
cruiser. "But the others were all here at the bar?
Could you swear to that in court?"

Vince's eyes widened behind his glasses. "Am
I going to court? Lady, I don't want to testify
against anybody. That's bad for business."

Derek put up a warning hand. "You boys keep
your distance. We don't want any trouble."

Denny snickered. "You're the only one making trouble, Johnson. Moving in on my brother's wife?"

"Ex-wife," Derek reminded him. "I only went
out with Vicki twice."

Jim Carlson moved within chest-bumping
distance. "That's two times too many as far as

we're concerned. You're taking advantage of my friend's unfortunate situation."

"Back off, Carlson," Derek warned. "Assaulting a police officer and impeding an investigation will land you back in jail."

"Were the others all here that afternoon, Mr. Goring?" Gina needed an answer. "Even Denny?"

Jim Carlson's skin reddened beneath the tats on his neck. But even as he wisely retreated a step, Denny slipped onto the barstool beside Gina, brushing his shoulder against hers. "You checking up on me, *querida*? I heard you weren't a cop no more."

Gina plucked her badge off her belt and slammed it on top of the bar in front of him. "Touch me one more time and I'll arrest you."

Derek held his ground behind her, but she heard the urgency in his tone. "G, we need to get moving."

Denny wiped his mouth, leaving a dot of spittle on his scraggly beard. "You think I shot you?"

"Doesn't seem like Vince here is much of an alibi. And I think your buddies are scared to say anything you don't want them to. Maybe you wanted revenge on us for arresting your brother? For me bossing you around? Or you were after Derek for dating Vicki, and I was collateral damage."

"And I shot all those other cops, too? Why

would I do that?" Denny snorted and reached for his flask. "I watch the news. I know you ain't the only cop who got hurt. As far as I know, ain't none of them boinking my brother's wife."

"That's enough, Bismarck," Derek warned him.

Bobby Estes was more likely to have premeditated the shooting, setting up the diversion of attacking other cops before going after her. The Bismarcks were heat-of-the-moment types of criminals. But she and Derek had been to the Bismarck house before on previous calls. Were these bozos smart enough to stage another assault on Vicki to set her and Derek up as targets? They sure seemed to have plenty of time on their hands to follow her to the physical therapy clinic or drive by her home or hang out here.

Denny had taken a swallow and tucked the flask back inside his jacket before Gina realized the place had gone quiet, except for the snoring coming from the end of the bar.

Gina backed away from the bar and surveyed the rest of the interior. There was nothing but a circle of abandoned coffee mugs at that back table now. "Where are your friends?"

Denny shrugged. "Al had to go back to work."

And she hadn't seen him leave. She clipped her badge onto her belt and pointed to Vince. "Is there a back door to this place?"

"Yeah."

She didn't know if she was madder at Derek for not telling her the men had slipped out or at herself for not noticing. She was damn certain she was mad at Denny for setting up the diversion while his comrades snuck out, knowing her suspicions were centered on him. "You could have left here that afternoon and come back to shoot up the Bismarck house without anyone seeing you leave."

Denny wasn't fazed by her brewing temper. "You saw me leave on my bike that day. Did you see me come back?"

She remembered the rusty old SUV with frozen, dirty slush thrown up around the wheel wells and masking the license plate. "You could have dropped your bike off here and come back in your '75 Bronco."

Gina held her ground when Denny stood and towered over her. "I could have, *querida*."

It didn't feel like a confession so much as a taunting reminder that she still had no answers. Only too many suspects with motives and opportunities.

The front door banged opened, flooding the bar with light. Gina squinted Mike's tall frame into focus. "Your ten minutes are up. We need to go."

"Mike—"

"Now." He sounded as if he'd just run a wind sprint. He backed out the open door, letting her know this wasn't that overprotective streak kicking in but something else.

She was smart enough to follow him. "Did you find something out?"

Denny's laughter confirmed her suspicion that he'd been diverting her attention for a reason. While Derek shoved him back onto his barstool and warned him to shut up, Gina hurried outside and ran to Mike's truck as he climbed in behind the wheel. "Mike?"

"That guy who was in the backseat of your cruiser the day I rescued you is leaving in a mighty big hurry." He turned the key in the ignition and shifted the pickup into Drive.

She was climbing onto the running board between the open door and frame of the truck, when she heard the growl of an engine revving up to full speed. When a big motorcycle roared out of the garage next door and jumped the curb before skidding into a sharp turn, Gina dropped into the passenger seat and slammed the door. "Go! Don't lose him."

Derek ran out of the bar behind her, shouting through the open window. "I'll call it in. If you get the plate number, let me know." Mike's tires spit up gravel before they found traction and they raced down the street after the motorcycle. "I suspect that place next door was a chop shop. They had an awful lot of car and motorcycle parts in the back room that belonged to high-end vehicles. Not the kind of stuff you see in this neighborhood."

Gina reached across the console to buckle him safely behind the wheel before sitting back to buckle herself in. "What were you doing in the back room?"

"Chasing the guy who ran in while you were next door asking questions."

"You were supposed to stick to getting your tires rotated." He was intent on dodging in and out of traffic and honking to warn pedestrians before they stepped into the street. Apparently, it was useless to argue the idea of staying away from danger with this man. "You're certain it was Gordon Bismarck? Big guy? Needs a haircut?"

He nodded, skidding his truck in a sharp right turn to follow the motorcycle around the corner. "The boss yelled 'Gordy' when he flew out of the garage. Thought that was a pretty good clue."

Gina frowned. Out of all the members of that aging biker gang, she'd figured Denny would be the one to come back and take potshots at the cops arresting his brother. She eyed the spinning lights of Derek's police car taking the corner behind them. Gina gripped the center console as Mike's truck sped through the next intersection. Denny was the one who should be running now. Was this chase the real diversion? Was Denny Bismarck slipping away into hiding right now?

"We should get back to the bar."

"You want me to turn this truck around?"

"Gordy Bismarck couldn't have shot me. He's the only one with an airtight alibi."

Mike skirted through another intersection as the light was turning red. "I'm staying on this guy's tail. Why run if he's got nothing to hide?"

Why wouldn't the answers she needed fall into place? "If that place was a chop shop for stolen car parts, then Gordy's violating his parole by being there. Maybe that's why he's running. It might not have anything to do with me."

"And it may have everything to do with you." Mike leaned on his horn and ran a second red light. "Maybe he knows who shot you and doesn't want you asking questions. Put a call through to my dad."

"I'm not calling in SWAT for a car chase." Gina's bottom left the seat as they bounced over a pothole. The motorcycle swerved around a delivery truck. Mike followed, nearly rear-ending the slow-moving car in front of it. "Look out!"

"I see it." He cut into the opposing lane of traffic, coming nose to nose with an oncoming bus.

"Mike!" He swerved at the last second, knocking Gina between the door and the console.

"You okay?"

"I'm fine. Just don't lose him." Her heart pounded against her ribs. "And don't do that again."

He steered his truck around another corner

and sped up the hill, trying to catch the racing motorcycle before it disappeared over the crest. "Call Dad and tell him to send somebody back to Sin City. We'll stay on this guy. And I want someone to know that we're chasing down a suspect. We're flying through town in an unmarked truck. Why hasn't anyone stopped *us* yet?"

They shot over the top of the hill and veered down the other side. Downtown traffic gave way to underpasses, railroad tracks and the warehouse district near the confluence of the Kansas and Missouri rivers. She should be seeing some neighborhood black-and-whites by now. Roads should be blocked off. A wary sense of unease that had nothing to do with the dangers of this daring thrill ride shivered down her spine. "Where's our backup?"

"Call Dad."

"Derek already called—"

"Your buddy Derek lost us after we nearly hit that bus. If we catch this guy, we'll need help. Call."

"What?!" But her partner's black-and-white wasn't in the rearview mirror. "Where…?"

"Call!"

She pulled out her phone and dialed Dispatch. "This is Officer Gina Galvan. I'm an off-duty cop." She gave her badge number and recited the partial license plate she'd gotten off the motorcycle, along with Gordon Bismarck's name and a description of the rider. "He's moving west on Twelfth. Suspect is in violation of his parole. I am in pursuit in a black pickup. Unit 4-13 has been notified of our intent and is also in pursuit. Although, I've lost sight of him. Please verify that he hasn't been in an accident."

"Acknowledged." The dispatcher's efficient monotone put out an APB over her headset before coming back on the line. "Notifying units in area of high-speed pursuit."

"No one's called this in yet?"

"I'm sending out a notification to all units now."

An all-call warning officers of the dangerous traffic situation in the area should have gone in five minutes ago. "What about sending a unit to the Sin City Bar?"

The dispatcher hesitated. "That's where Frank McBride was shot."

"Yes. I was questioning suspects there."

"My records show there's already a unit assigned to watch the bar."

"What?" She hadn't seen any police car in the area. "Then call them."

"Unit 4-13 was assigned that duty this morning. 10:00 a.m. to 2:00 p.m."

"4-13 is with me." Only he wasn't. Gina inhaled a deep breath, quashing her emotions. "I need you to send a new unit to Sin City Bar to round up Denny Bismarck, Al Renken, Jim Carlson and Aldo Pitsaeli for questioning. And send an alert to Michael Cutler of SWAT Team One that his son is with me."

"Copy that. Unit dispatched. Message sent."

"Galvan out." Gina's phone tumbled out of her hand as they bounced over a railroad crossing and followed the motorcycle into the West Bottoms area of the city. Once a teeming center of commerce, the monoliths of rusting metal and sagging brick walls stood like looming sentinels beside the river. Although much of the district had been bought by investors and was slowly being transformed into trendy art houses, antique shops and reception halls, the buildings were only open on weekends. In the middle of the week, there were only a few lone cars on the streets, and one small moving van backed up against a concrete loading dock.

It should have made it easy to spot Gordy. But he'd steered the more maneuverable motorcycle up and down side streets and alleys, and they'd lost him. Mike slowed his speed as they drove down Wyoming Street, each checking every alleyway and open warehouse door on their side of the street.

"Where did he go?" Gina heard the distant sound of police sirens a split second before she heard the familiar sound of an engine revving. When Gordy shot out of the cross street in front of them, Mike floored the accelerator. "There he is!"

"Hold on!" Mike's big pickup left the stink of burned rubber behind them as he took a hard turn to the left.

Gina spotted the wall of chain link fence and piles of plastic trash bags stacked between it and the food truck at the loading dock behind a café where two men were hauling out crates of produce. "Blind alley!"

Mike stomped on the brakes. Gina's shoulder protested bracing her hands against the dashboard. The truck skidded to an abrupt halt while Gordy gunned his bike up the concrete ramp to leap the security fence. But he hit a dolly loaded with lettuce and tomatoes and spun out. The bike crashed into the fence and Gordy rolled across the concrete, sliding off the edge into the bundles of trash.

Before Gina could get unbuckled, pull out her badge and warn the two workers to stay inside the café, Mike was out of the truck, racing down the alley toward Gordy Bismarck as he scrambled to his feet. But his limping gait didn't stand a chance against Mike's long legs. Gordy abandoned his bike and was halfway up the fence when Mike leaped up, grabbed the other man and pulled him down. They tumbled into a sea of restaurant waste, but Mike had Gordy's face pressed against the pavement by the time Gina caught up to them.

"KCPD!" she announced. "Stay on the ground!"

Mike was breathing hard from the exertion. But given Gordy's deep gasps, and pale, oxygen-deprived skin, she knew Mike clearly had the upper hand. Still, Gina wasn't about to trust any perp's cooperation at this point. After a quick assessment of their surroundings, she shut off the motorcycle's engine and pulled the strapping tape from one of the broken crates to wind it around Gordy's wrists, securing him and checking his pockets for any weapons before she gave Mike the okay to release him.

"I'm getting tired of arresting you, Gordy. Why did you run from us?" Gina demanded, stowing the pocketknife she'd found on him before rolling him over and showing him her badge.

When he didn't immediately answer, Mike grabbed him by the shoulders of his jacket and sat him up against the fence to face her. "Answer Officer Galvan's question."

"I'm not going back to prison," he answered on a toneless breath.

"You will if you shot a cop," Mike reminded him, his usually friendly voice low and menacing. "We were just there to ask questions. You look guilty making us chase you all over town."

Gordy tilted his gaze up to Mike, evaluating his younger, fitter, more ready-to-do-battle posture before deciding to talk to Gina. "I didn't shoot you, lady. You know I didn't. Hell, I was in the backseat of your car. I got shot at, too."

"But you didn't get hit. You were protected while my partner and I were out in the open. What about Officer McBride?"

"Who?"

"The cop who was wounded yesterday at Sin City."

Silence.

Mike tugged Gordy forward by the collar of his jacket. "Do you know who shot Gina?"

Gordy glared at Mike but didn't answer.

Refusing to speak wasn't an option as far as Gina was concerned. "Did Denny come back to the house to shoot us? Is that why you ran? To protect your brother the way he protected you that day? Or are you just worried about you and your boys getting caught working in a chop shop?"

She must have struck a nerve with one of those questions because Gordy's gaze dropped to the pavement. "I want my attorney."

Gina turned at the blare of sirens at the end of the alley as two black-and-whites pulled up. Two officers climbed out of the first car, one radioing in the situation report, while the other hurried over with a proper pair of handcuffs to secure Bismarck and drag him to his feet.

Gordy looked down at Gina. "A man's got a right to protect what's his."

Was he confessing a motive for the shooting? Or was he defending his actions to protect his brother?

While the officer led Bismarck to the backseat of the cruiser, Derek jogged around the corner. "G? You all right?"

Her voice was sharp when he reached her. "Just how many times did you sleep with Vicki Bismarck?"

"Whoa." Derek put up his hands, stopping just short of touching her. "That came out of left field."

"Not really. Gordy and Denny seem to think you're a motive for their behavior. Beating up on Vicki. Threatening us. Maybe even firing a gun at us. Because you moved in on Gordy's woman."

Derek propped his hands at his waist, alternately smiling and looking as if he was about to cuss up a blue streak. "That is out of line, G. Bismarck's got no claim on her. They're divorced. And I told you, I went out with her twice."

"The Bismarcks seem to think it was more than that."

"The Bismarcks are wrong. Whose side are you on, anyway?"

Gina shook her head. "You should have recused yourself from that interview this morning."

The smile didn't win. "Hey, you were the one who called me for the favor."

"That was my mistake. My second mistake was counting on you to help me round up Bismarck." She took two steps toward Mike's truck and spun around to face Derek. "Where were you? What if he'd gotten away?"

"I circled around to Thirteenth to cut him off when I lost you. I thought he was heading for the interstate. How was I to know he'd do a U-ee and head toward the river?"

"What about sealing off traffic corridors and keeping everyone else safe while we were in pursuit of a suspect? I called Dispatch myself."

"I called it in," he insisted.

"When? Dispatch hadn't gotten your call yet."

"So it wasn't the first thing I did. I was focused on driving. Everybody has an off day."

An off day? She was done with him settling for being an average cop who lived by an ambiguous moral code.

"You should have stuck to stakeout duty at the bar." He'd have to be blind not to read the disappointment screaming from her body language. She marched back to Mike's truck, aware that Derek was hurrying after her.

"I'll go back to the bar and round the Bismarcks up for questioning."

Gina waved off the offer and kept walking. "Already taken care of. If they're not long gone."

"Did you want me to take care of *them*? Or take care of *you*?"

Gina whirled around on him. "I don't need to be taken care of. I need you to do your job."

He thumped his chest. "I'm the one still wearing a uniform."

Gina shoved her fingers through her hair, muttering a curse, before inhaling a deep breath so she could speak calmly. "Well then, Mr. Uniform, notify the auto-theft team that that place next door to Sin City may be housing stolen vehicle parts. If Denny and his gang haven't cleared them out already."

"Stop giving me orders, G. Look, it's not like we were chasing some piece-of-junk Chevy."

"Why would we—?"

"You were after a guy on a motorcycle. A wild-goose chase that steps on the toes of some other department's investigation. You've got me running errands and filing reports on KCPD time, when I'm supposed to be doing my job at the Precinct." He gestured to the empty belt at her waist. "You're not even cleared to wear your gun, much less run your own investigation. I'm the one trying to cover your backside so you don't get in trouble with the brass."

"Me?"

"Yeah. Haven't you heard? My dad talked to a lawyer about suing you and the department for allowing me to get shot."

"Allowing…?" She'd suspected as much. Didn't stop her temper from flaring. "He has no case. There is only one person responsible for you and me and Frank and Colin getting shot. I'm doing everything I can to find this guy before he shoots someone else—before he kills one of us. I thought that was what you wanted, too." She turned toward the truck, then faced Derek one last time. "And why would you say 'piece-of-junk Chevy'? Are you remembering something from the shooting? Did you see the shooter's vehicle?"

That seemed to genuinely take him aback, knocking the anger out of his voice and posture. "What? I don't think so. It's just a figure of speech."

"No, it's not."

She was aware that Mike had followed them and spoken briefly to the officers in the first police cruiser to arrive on the scene. It wasn't the hole ripped into the knee of his jeans or the unidentifiable glop of food staining the sleeve of his shirt or even the subtle limp she detected in his stride that proved he'd gone above and beyond to protect her and help track down the man who might hold the key to the truth. Now he circled to his side of the truck, giving her some space to deal with her partner. But his watchful blue eyes never left her. He was ready to intervene if she needed him—and willing to step back if she didn't. *That* was the kind of backup she expected from anyone she called *partner*.

But Derek just didn't get it. He didn't understand fire and dedication and getting the job done the way she did. "G, you're a little obsessed. Maybe we're never going to catch the guy who shot us. Maybe we just need to move on. I can handle my dad. You need to go home and heal. We need to focus on keeping our noses clean and making SWAT."

She shrugged off his placating touch and climbed in beside Mike. "You quit if you want, Derek. I never will."

Chapter Eleven

"Here's a clean shirt from my locker, son." Mike caught the black KCPD polo his father tossed to him and straightened away from the wall outside the Fourth Precinct's third-floor conference room as several more officers, both uniformed and plainclothes, filed out of the room behind him and moved on down the hallway to their various work stations. Michael Sr. wrinkled his nose at the stain on Mike's shoulder, which could be the remnants of spoiled pasta sauce or a really old tomato. "You're a little fragrant."

"Thanks, Dad." Ignoring the protest from joints that weren't used to duking it out with armed bullies or tackling a man off a concrete loading dock, Mike unbuttoned his soiled shirt and shrugged into the clean one. "What's the verdict?"

Although the captain was just *Dad* to Mike, Gina hurried over from pacing up and down the hallway and practically snapped to attention. "What can you tell us, sir? Did Gordy Bismarck say anything else after lawyering up? No one else was hurt during that chase, were they? What about Denny Bismarck? Did we find him?"

The Precinct's top brass and investigators from various departments had been called in for a briefing on everything that had happened between the confrontation at Gina's home last night to the Sin City Bar and stopping Gordon Bismarck in a pile of trash near the river this morning. Michael Sr. splayed his fingers at the waist of his dark uniform, looking down at her with a boss-like seriousness. "Denny Bismarck has gone to ground, but there's a citywide APB out on him. We've got unis checking their regular haunts. We've arrested Al Renken on trafficking stolen goods and Gordy on his parole violation and resisting arrest."

"Even though I was the officer in pursuit?" A worried frown marred Gina's beautiful eyes. "Technically, I'm still on leave. The arrest is good? Am I going on report?"

Mike felt the same paternal, perhaps reprimanding, glare fixed on him for a moment before his father answered Gina's concern. "You're still KCPD. You identified yourself with your badge—Bismarck said as much. Your instincts were good about the Bismarcks and their buddies hiding something. The auto-theft team wants to buy you a drink down at the Shamrock for breaking one of their investigations wide open. I think I've got some competition for recruiting you."

The compliment didn't seem to register. "But I'm no closer to finding out who's shooting cops."

"None of us are." The grim pronouncement hung in the stuffy hallway air. "But there are a lot of officers in there who'd like to get Denny in an interrogation room. I'm confident we'll figure this out."

Gina rubbed her shoulder through her denim jacket. Mike wondered if she was in pain, or if that was becoming a habit of the self-doubts and second-guessing that were new to her. "Hopefully, before anyone else gets hurt."

He agreed with a nod. "We're all working this case, Gina. When you attack one cop, you attack all of us. You and Mike have given the detectives several leads to follow up on, including your buddy Bobby Estes. But you need to step back and let Detectives Grove and Kincaid take the lead on this. Go home. You've earned a good night's rest. We'll get this guy. I promise."

"Yes, sir."

Michael's face relaxed into a smile for Gina. "Mind if I borrow my son for a moment?"

Gina's dark gaze darted up to Mike's. "I didn't mean to get him into trouble, Captain. No one's issuing Mike a reckless driving ticket, are they? If I'd been able to drive myself—"

The captain raised a reassuring hand. "Mike's

a grown man. It's kind of hard to reprimand him. But we decided not to issue any tickets since he was assisting a police officer." It probably didn't hurt that he was Michael Cutler's son, either. "We do, however, have some things to discuss. Personal things."

But Mike could see his father's explanation had only made Gina straighten to a more defensive posture. Defending him? Or worried that causing friction between father and son would further jeopardize her chances of making the new SWAT team?

"This is nothing for you to stress over," Mike assured her. "We're just two guys having a conversation."

"I'll give you some privacy then." Gina reached over to brush her limp fingers against his knuckles before turning her hand into his and squeezing it. The gesture was shyly hesitant—if he could believe anything about this brave, direct woman could be shy—but it meant the world to Mike. Was that an apology for getting him into any kind of trouble? A thank-you? Maybe her only hesitation was that she was confirming the connection between them in front of his father. "I want to read over my statement again before I sign it. I'll be downstairs in the lobby when you're finished."

"I'll find you there."

He watched her cross to her desk in the main

room, pick up the printout of the statement she'd typed earlier and sit down to read it before his father nodded toward the break room. "Buy you a cup of coffee?"

Mike followed his dad inside and closed the door, although he questioned the privacy of this conversation since the walls on either side of the door were glass windows with open blinds hanging in front of them. "*Personal* things?"

When had his dad gone all touchy-feely?

His father pulled out a couple of insulated paper cups and poured them both some hot coffee. "The auto-theft team impounded Denny Bismarck's '75 Bronco. They'd like you to look at it to see if you recognize it from that day at the shooting."

"Not a problem." He took the cup from his dad. "Let's hear the real reason you wanted to talk without Gina around. You think I'm getting in too deep with this. Too deep with her."

"She's getting her grip back?"

He wasn't surprised that his dad had noticed the way Gina had reached for his hand. "I don't know if it'll ever be one hundred percent, probably not steady enough to hold a sniper rifle. But I still wouldn't count her out in a fight. She's already good enough to pass her competency exam on the shooting range."

"Have you told her that?" His dad arched a

questioning brow. "I need better than competent for SWAT."

Mike took a sip of the steaming brew, thinking the bitter sludge beat Frannie's coffee but wasn't anywhere near the smooth delight Lupe Molina's coffee had been. But he knew this conversation wasn't about father-son bonding or evaluating caffeinated drinks. This was Captain Michael Cutler, KCPD, asking for a report on the recovery of a wounded police officer he wanted to recruit. "She's still a good cop. You haven't seen her out in the field, Dad. She's fearless. Gina knows how to handle herself in an interview. She's got good instincts about protecting people. And she's kind and strong and inspiring with the victims I've seen her talk to."

"She wants to be SWAT. Not a victim's advocate."

"She wants to be a cop."

His father nodded, considering the update on Gina's progress. He took a drink before changing the subject. "How do you figure into all this? Are you looking to be a cop now, too?"

Mike chuckled, hearing the fatherly concern about risking his life, yet knowing exactly from what gene pool he'd inherited this strong urge to help others and protect the people he cared about. "That's your calling, Dad. Not mine. Business has been slow at the clinic, so I've had time on my hands. Gina's going to chase this guy down whether or not she has anyone watching her back. I prefer she not take on the whole world alone and aggravate her injury before she's completely healed." He shrugged, instantly regretting the twinge through the stretching muscles of his back. "I help out where I can."

"Driving eighty miles an hour through downtown Kansas City is your idea of helping out? I didn't know your big dream was to drive for NASCAR one day."

Nah. His big dream was to find the man who'd shot Gina so that she'd give up this crazy investigation and give them a chance at being a couple. "I couldn't lose that guy, Dad. He knows something that could help her. For all we know, he's the key to stopping whoever is targeting cops. Or who might be targeting Gina specifically. That's a theory we're working on."

"A theory?" Those observant blue eyes, so like his own, narrowed, no doubt suspecting the pain he was in. "You look a little beat-up yourself. Fractured nerves and steel pins doing okay?"

Mike admitted to the electric shocks sparking intermittently through his lower back and the ache in his right leg that had been numb when they'd left the crime scene earlier. "I've had better days. Some ibuprofen and a hot shower ought to take care of it."

"I wanted you to help Gina get fit enough to come back to KCPD—not for you to get caught in the cross fire. I nearly lost you once." He wandered over to peer through the blinds beside Mike. "Trip and Alex told me about the run-in at Gina's place last night. Your truck never left the driveway. Just how serious has it gotten between you two?"

"We've become friends." Standing beside his father and fingering the visitor's badge hanging around his neck, Mike studied the main room. More accurately, he studied the dark-haired woman at the far end of the sea of desks between them. Gina methodically read through the printout, making notations. "I was giving her a break from having to be responsible for her family, her neighborhood, this whole city for one night. She's such a tiny thing, and yet she carries the weight of the world on her shoulders." Mike grinned, trying to make light of the truth his father was no doubt reading between the lines. "And her great-aunt Lupe sure can cook. Her coffee's a damn sight better than this stuff."

The joke didn't work. He felt his father's hand on his shoulder. "You are never going to be so old that I won't worry about you. If she's using you to get into SWAT—"

"Gina wouldn't know how." Mike pulled away from his father's hand and poured out the last of his coffee into the sink before dropping the cup into the trash. "She's honest to a fault, Dad. Good, bad or ugly. She says what she means, and anything she gets she wants to earn on her own merit."

"I thought as much. But I had to ask."

Mike headed to the door, thinking this tête-à-tête was over. But before he turned the knob, he saw Derek Johnson perch on the corner of Gina's desk. She tipped her head up to her partner as they chatted, then pushed to her feet as the conversation grew heated. Derek pointed toward the break room, and Mike had to wonder if the disagreement had to do with him or his father. But whatever they were arguing about ended quickly. Gina tucked her report into a file folder and carried it over to Kevin Grove and Atticus Kincaid, the detectives leading the investigation, and dropped it on Grove's desk. Mike glanced back to her desk to see Derek watching her, too. When she excused herself and headed to the elevators, Derek sank into his chair, slumping like a pouting boy. He wasn't thrilled with whatever she'd said or written. Gina had disappeared around the last cubicle wall by the time he sat forward and picked up the phone on his desk, punching in a number as if an idea had suddenly entered his head.

Mike was about to overstep a line with his father, taking advantage of his KCPD connections. "Dad, I know you're not an investigator, but could you check out Derek Johnson for me?"

"Gina's partner?"

Mike wondered how much of that argument he'd just witnessed had to do with the accusations she'd made that morning after the car chase through downtown. "I've seen rookies who make fewer dumb moves than that guy does. It's almost like he's sabotaging anything Gina tries to do. I wonder if he blames her for getting shot."

"That's a serious accusation. Not every partnership works out," his father conceded. "Maybe there is some tension between them—especially if someone was targeting her and he feels like collateral damage. Or vice versa. I heard about his fling with Bismarck's wife. But his work history is clean. He came recommended to me for SWAT training, so I know he hasn't been written up for anything."

"What kind of cop do you think he is?"

Michael Sr. considered his answer before speaking. "He's in the top half of every test I've given him. He takes orders. Does what I ask of him in training. He gets along with everybody on the team."

"What about his personal life?"

"I don't know him that well, but I can poke around. No one will question me looking more closely at any of the SWAT candidates. What am I looking for?"

They both watched the animated phone call as Derek smacked the desktop and argued with whoever was on the other end of the line. "I'm not sure. I can't put my finger on it. But something's hinky with that guy. I don't think Gina trusts him any more than I do. Maybe that's one reason she's so damn independent. She doesn't believe Johnson's got her back."

"But you do?" His father crumpled the empty coffee cup and tossed it into the trash. "Need I remind you, you don't wear a uniform? You've got no responsibility here. Gina has a whole police department she can call on for help. Last I checked, putting your life on the line for a woman in trouble isn't part of a physical therapist's job description. You took on Leo Mesner when he was hitting Frannie. Caroline's parents were controlling every aspect of her life until you..." He saw realization dawn in his father's sharp blue eyes. "You're in love with her. Mike, I wasn't matchmaking when I asked you to help—"

"This isn't like Caroline or Frannie, Dad." He didn't need to be reminded of his past mistakes. "They needed a support system—someone who would put their needs first."

"Isn't that what you're doing for Gina?"

"She won't let me half the time." He laughed, but there was no humor in the sound. "She was a fighter before I ever met her. Strong and confident. This injury is just a temporary setback until she figures out a new way to move forward. That spirit is still inside her. She doesn't need me to hold her hand or build up her ego, she just… needs me. For how long, I don't know yet, but—"

"I like Gina well enough." His father looked him straight in the eye, wanting him to really hear what he was saying. "Whatever you decide, you know I'll back you all the way. But I don't want to see you get hurt again."

Yeah, the pattern of Mike's woeful love life did seem to be repeating itself. Maybe he was the one who needed to be rescued from the mistakes he kept making. But not yet. He wasn't giving up on Gina or his feelings for her. "She says she doesn't have the time or space in her life for a relationship right now. But everything in me says that she's the one. That we could be really good together if she'd give us a chance."

"From what I've seen, she cares about you. But caring isn't the same as—"

"Just check Johnson out for me, okay? If his partner can't rely on him or his priorities are somewhere else besides his job… She doesn't need that right now."

"That kind of behavior is troubling when it comes to building a SWAT team, too." With a nod, his father became a cop again. "I hope you're wrong. But I'll see what I can find out. I'll give you a call the moment we take Denny Bismarck into custody, too. In the meantime, keep your head down. I'm not explaining it to Jillian and Will if you get hurt again."

"Thanks, Dad." He pushed open the break-room door to go after Gina and run interference between her and Derek if she needed it.

"Mike?" He stopped and turned as his dad caught the door behind him. He turned for one last piece of paternal advice. "Falling for your stepmother was a complete surprise for me. I thought I was done with love until Jillian came along. And then I nearly lost her."

"I know Jillian's been good for you, Dad. She's been good for all of us. Hell, she's the one who finally got me up out of that wheelchair. She made our family complete."

"If Gina's the one, you need to be a fighter, too." That was the voice of experience that Mike took to heart. "Fight for her with everything you've got."

"I intend to."

WHY THE HECK were they running the air conditioning this early in the spring? Maybe it was the cold marble walls of the Precinct's first-floor lobby that made Gina shiver. But looking through the reinforced glass and steel-framed doors, she still saw more brown than green in the grass outside. And even without a cloud in the sky, the afternoon sun couldn't quite seem to reach her skin through the glass.

She was practical enough to know the chill

came from a place inside her. But as to its cause? Where to begin?

She worried that she'd gotten Mike into trouble with his dad by involving him in this private investigation into the cop shootings, along with the rest of her screwed-up life. Not that she'd invited him to be a part of any of it. But now she couldn't imagine *not* having Mike around as her chauffeur, friend, sounding board, protector and catnip. On paper, he was every kind of wrong for her. Wrong background. Wrong neighborhood. Wrong skin color.

But in reality, everything between them felt right. Gina shook her head. How could she ever make a reality with Mike work? Chemistry alone couldn't sustain a relationship. Their personalities clashed. Her family was a responsibility she would never give up. His father might be her boss one day. But the thought of Mike Cutler not holding her for another night, or never kissing her again or never even butting heads with her made her feel empty. And cold.

Maybe the lack of warmth stemmed from the fact that she'd probably irreparably damaged her relationship with Derek by promising to report his less-than-stellar performance on the job to their superior officer and Captain Cutler if he didn't get off his lazy butt and start doing his job the way they'd been trained at the academy. Today she'd been reminded that, technically, it wasn't her job to solve this case. But she knew they could find the shooter if they stayed sharp and ran down every lead. Maybe she'd called in one favor too many, and Derek was right to be angry about helping her. But why couldn't he have just told her *no* instead of stringing her along with his half-hearted assistance? When had they stopped being able to trust each other and communicate like partners should? Maybe Derek had moved on from the shooting. But she needed closure. She needed to know why someone had wanted to change her life so irreparably.

Maybe those answers would finally erase the sense that an enemy was watching, circling, drawing ever closer. And she wouldn't be able to recognize him until it was too late.

Gina moved closer to the rays of sunlight streaming in through the windows and rubbed her hand up and down the sleeve of her jacket while she waited for her great-aunt or -uncle to pick up the phone.

Knowing how slowly Lupe and Rollo moved, she waited patiently through several rings. Still, she breathed an audible sigh of relief when her great-aunt picked up. "*Hola*, Gina."

"*Hola*, Tia Mami." Some of the pervading chill left at the cheerful sound of Lupe's voice. She was glad to hear that someone in her family was having a good day. "I'm calling to see if you're all okay after last night. Mike and I had to leave before everyone was up. Did Sylvie get to school okay?"

"*Sí*. I let her drive the car so she wouldn't have to call Bobby. She wore blue jeans and looked like a teenage girl. So pretty."

"Good." Hopefully, her sister would be smart enough to come straight home after school, too, even if Bobby tried to contact her. "And Tio Papi? How's his blood pressure?"

"He is taking it easy today. He found the Royals playing a preseason game on television. Javier is watching with him." She could hear the laughter in Lupe's voice. "In truth, they are both napping. They wake up when there's a big play."

The gentle normalcy of such a report made Gina smile, too. "And you're checking Papi's pressure every hour?"

"He fusses at me. But I remind him that Mike said to do so, and he stops arguing with me."

Gina's attention shifted and her smile faded when Harold Johnson, Derek's father, loped up the front steps. The fringe of his brown leather jacket bounced with every stride. Since they were both on their cell phones, intent on their own conversations, Gina turned away from the door, letting the people milling through the lobby and Harold's hurry to get to the elevators prevent him from seeing her. She'd already had enough unpleasant conversations today. Did he really think he had a legal case against her? Was the idea of suing her and the department on Derek's behalf just his way of showing his son he cared? Or were the accusations an idle man's latest idea on how to get some easy money, as Derek claimed? Should she be worried that he was running upstairs to see Derek now?

Gina gradually tuned back in to Lupe's list of errands she needed to run when Sylvie or she got home. "Will Mike be coming to the house again tonight? Should I set him a place for dinner? He has a good appetite, that one."

"Tia Mami…" Suddenly, Harold Johnson's reflection loomed up behind her in the front window. So much for avoiding unpleasant conversations.

"I know, I know. He is not your boyfriend. But he could be. You are being nice to him, yes?"

A shiver ran down her spine like a wintry omen. But having Derek's father intrude on her personal phone call only made Gina stand up straighter. She turned to face him, keeping her voice calm even as she felt the glass behind her back and knew she was trapped. "I have to go. I'll call you later. *Te amo.*"

Harold flipped his oily, gray ponytail behind his back and leaned in toward her. *"Hola, traidor."*

Traitor. Gina tilted her chin, refusing to be insulted or intimidated. "Mr. Johnson."

"I just got off the phone with Derek. Just because you got crippled up doesn't make it fair to file a complaint about my boy."

Crippled up? Is that how Harold saw her? Gina glanced around either side of his worn jacket, wondering if anyone else—maybe the two men coming off the elevators, maybe the elderly couple chatting with a public information officer at the front desk, maybe Derek or even Captain Cutler—saw her as crippled, too. Her damaged hand curled into a fist down at her side, the only outward sign that anything Harold Johnson said could get to her. "Mr. Johnson, you need to take a step back. You're in my personal space."

"Is that so?" If anything, he moved closer.

"Maybe you shouldn't be talking to me. Especially if you're filing a lawsuit. Derek told me. You know what part of town I live in. Even if you had a case, you wouldn't get any money out of me." More than anything, she wanted to shove him back a step. But she suspected turning this battle of wills into a physical confrontation would only add fuel to his irrational fire. "Maybe you should be supporting your son, encouraging him to be a better police officer, instead of making excuses for him or blaming other people when things go wrong."

"Ooh, now the pretty little *chica*'s got her dander up." Harold placed his hand on the window beside her head, smudging the glass. His clothes smelled of grease and dust and had the burnt odor of acetylene from the blow torch he must use at the junkyard to disassemble cars, appliances and old construction materials into scrap metal. Not that she had anything against a hardworking man, but she doubted this lifelong schemer and champion of political incorrectness qualified. "I talked to a lawyer. I'm going to prove my boy is a better cop than you are."

"You're doing it to make a buck and retire at the department's expense. Think about Derek's reputation. No one is going to want to partner with him if they're afraid you're going to sue them over any grievance or mistake they make."

"You admit you made a mistake that got my boy shot?"

She was admitting nothing. Harold could twist the truth any way he wanted, but Gina knew there was only one person to blame for her and Derek's injuries—the gunman who'd fired those bullets. "Your son will get the job on SWAT if he earns it. If someone else is more deserving, then they will be put on the new team."

"Like you?" He snorted and backed away. "You immigrants are all alike." *Immigrant?* She and her siblings had been born right here in Kansas City. Not that it was worth arguing that point with a man who wouldn't listen. "Thinking you're entitled to something just because you're a girl or a minority. If you've done anything to hurt Derek's chances of that promotion—"

"Dad." The stairwell door off to Gina's right closed behind Derek as he strolled over to join them. "You need to back off before you get me into more trouble."

Harold ignored his son's stern warning. "No. If she can't do the job, she can't do it. She needs to step aside and let a man take her place on the team."

The stairwell door opened a second time, and Mike entered the lobby. He strode straight to Gina, made no apology for nudging Derek aside, reached for her hand and pulled her away from the window and uncomfortable closeness of Derek's father. "Everything okay?"

He'd followed Derek. He'd probably been suspicious of her partner taking the stairs instead of coming down on the elevator. Why was Derek here, anyway? He should still be on duty. Was he following her? Did he know his dad had her cornered down here? Had he summoned his dad to do just that? Or was he truly worried about his father making his situation worse by showing up here?

Gina squeezed Mike's hand, glad for the subtle show of support. "I'm fine. Mr. Johnson was just expressing an opinion. I disagreed."

Derek propped his hand on his father's shoulder, uniting them as a team, too. "Gina never gives up, Dad. She made that perfectly clear." He turned that smug, mocking smile on her. "Well, you should know, G, that I don't, either. I deserve to be on that SWAT team. I'm the one who's still training with them every week. I'm the one going on calls with them." He cupped his arm where he'd been shot. "I'm the decorated cop who's returned to duty. When Captain Cutler posts the list, I'll be on it." He snorted through his nose, sounding just like his father. "You'll still be on medical leave. Unless you think sleeping with your boyfriend here will get you that SWAT badge. I can't compete with that."

Gina felt the instant tension of Mike moving forward. She latched on to him with both hands and held him back. "*Not* my bodyguard," she whispered against his shoulder. "If anybody's going to punch this guy, I want it to be me. You'd better get me out of here."

Chapter Twelve

Gina scooped up the last handful of bubbles in her wrinkled fingers and blew them across the top of the water. She should feel guilty for stepping away from her responsibilities for any length of time. But technically, she was following orders.

Captain Cutler had told her to take the night off. Give other officers a chance to do their job. Mike had told her she needed to rest, that she'd been pushing herself physically more than he thought wise at this stage of her recovery. And since that was the only thing he'd said during the first ten minutes of their drive after pulling out of the KCPD parking garage across from headquarters, she was quick to agree.

Mike's silence wasn't something she was accustomed to. No comment on her stowing her gun and badge in the glove compartment of his truck. No admonishment over pushing so hard on this investigation that they could have both been injured or killed more than once. No explanation for how she'd been ordered to stand down by a superior officer—Mike's own father—and then Mike was the one who'd been taken aside for a private conversation.

A few weeks ago, she would have relished not having him tell her what she could and couldn't do. She would have been more than happy for him to drop an argument when she suggested he do so. But now, after spending so much time together, after drawing on the strength and support of a true friend, after developing these feelings that went beyond friendship—feelings which she was certain would get her into trouble somewhere along the way—his silence worried her. Was Mike angry? Deep in thought? Worried about something he didn't want to share? Did this have to do with the insults Derek had slung at her? Frustration with the investigation? Was he in pain?

Why would the man who prodded her about everything suddenly go silent?

When she'd admitted that she'd like to wash up before dinner, Mike had responded with a simple, "Me, too." Although she hadn't taken the brunt of the garbage outside the West Bottoms café this morning, she felt soiled and slimy just from her conversations with Denny and Gordy Bismarck, and then with Derek and his father.

A quick cleanup and fresh change of clothes sounded wonderful.

She thought he'd take her to her house. Or maybe once he'd charmed the socks off her great-aunt during a quick phone call, saying not to hold dinner for them but that they'd be there for dessert, she thought Mike was taking her out to eat someplace, making the break his father had ordered them to take sound very much like a date. She wouldn't have complained if that had been his plan.

But Mike Cutler knew her far better than she'd realized. They drove through a burger joint for takeout and ate in the truck before ending up at his ranch-style home in the suburbs. The neighborhood was quiet except for the kids playing a game of hide and seek across the street. Traffic was light. There weren't cars parked bumper-to-bumper at the curb. The yards were well tended and, though they had mature trees, the street itself was wide, allowing plenty of late afternoon sun through to warm her skin as she tipped her face up to the sky and breathed deeply.

The house itself needed a little work—probably why a single man struggling to make his fledgling business a success could afford to buy a home here—but the space was more than double the size of the home she shared with her family. The fenced-in backyard was made for barbecues and swing sets and gardens. And even though much of the house was stuck in the 1970s or was in the process of being remodeled, he showed her three different bathrooms where she could freshen up.

Three bathrooms. Heaven.

Other than the green and gold of the '70s decor, this place was everything she wanted for her family. It was as suburban and perfect and interestingly unexpected as Mike himself was.

When the tour was finished, Mike left her with a fresh towel and new bar of soap in the tiny powder room off the modern white kitchen. "Make yourself at home. I'll take a fast shower. If you get hungry or want something to drink, help yourself to whatever you can find in the fridge."

While she liked the retro look of the new black and white tiles and nickel-finish faucet, the pedestal sink just wasn't calling to her. "Do I have to use this bathroom?"

Mike shrugged. "I haven't had time or money to remodel the guest bathroom in the hallway yet."

"But it has a bathtub. Could I…?" She tilted her face up to his. "Instead of just washing my face here, would it be a horrible imposition if I took a bath?"

"And I thought *I* was your catnip." Mike smiled at her request. Really smiled. Then he dipped his head to capture her mouth in a kiss that heated her blood but left her little time to respond. Instead, he turned her around, gently swatting her bottom to nudge her down the hallway into the guest bathroom. "Towels are in the cabinet. Some of my little brother's bubble bath, too, if you want. Enjoy yourself."

"I'm sure I will. Thanks."

He closed the door. She heard the shower running in his own bathroom off the master bedroom before she turned on the faucets in the tub to let it fill while she quickly shed her clothes.

She was still lounging in the tub when the shower next door stopped. Gina checked the time on her phone on the towel shelf beside the tub where she'd stowed her folded clothes. Fifteen minutes. She sighed in contentment, closing her eyes and leaning her head back against the tub wall. She hadn't relaxed like this in weeks, months maybe.

This was no five-minute shower and dash to her bedroom to dry her hair so that someone else could get into the bathroom. This was fifteen minutes of pure heaven, soaking in a bubble bath. Even the fruity smell of the child's soap bubbles couldn't diminish the dreamy satisfaction of hot water turning every muscle into goo and the delicious quiet of long-term solitude, interrupted only by an occasional dribble of water as she shifted position.

Had anyone ever pampered her like this? She was a warrior. A protector in every sense of the word. No one ever saw the girly-girl inside her. Had anyone outside of her family ever cared enough to indulge her feminine side? Growing up in a life so full of need, had she ever opened herself up enough to allow an outsider to know her foolish secrets? It was a little unsettling to admit that Mike knew her like that. When had she allowed herself to become so vulnerable to a man? Why wasn't she more frightened by the inherent risk of allowing a man to see her as a woman? Not a cop. Not a big sister or neighborhood protector or family breadwinner. Not a patient or even a friend.

With Mike Cutler, aka Choir Boy and Mr. Nice Guy, of all people—she felt like a woman.

Gina heard a whisper of sound from the doorway behind her.

Make that a desirable woman.

She'd been so deep in thought that she hadn't heard Mike open the door. "I knocked. You've been in here so long and it was so quiet that, when you didn't answer, I'd thought I'd better check to see you hadn't fallen asleep in the tub and drowned."

"Sorry to worry you. But I'm fine." She crossed her arms over her chest, inhaling a satisfied breath. "More than fine, actually."

"Very fine, from this angle." Mike shifted, leaning his shoulder against the door jamb. From the corner of her eye, she could see he'd only been out of the shower long enough to towel off and pull on his jeans. Droplets of water still glistened in the dark spikes of his hair. He'd trimmed his beard back to sexy perfection.

The only bubbles that remained were clinging to the edge of the tub. Gina smiled, not feeling the water's cooling temperature at all. If anything, her temperature was rising. "A nice guy wouldn't stand there staring."

"Told you I wasn't a nice guy."

She found his gaze, dark blue and unabashedly focused on her, in the mirror. The message she read there was crystal clear, and it thrilled her down to her very core. Last night, the timing had been off. She'd been emotionally exhausted and worried about her family. But this evening was a different story. There weren't family members here they had to tiptoe around. Other cops were handling the bad guys tonight. And Mike had been so sullen earlier, to see him engaged and talking again like the man she'd gotten to know made her want to savor this charged moment. "How are your hips and legs? Did the hot shower help?"

"I'm okay."

"Okay enough to climb in this tub with me?" she invited.

Mike walked over to the tub, holding out his hand to her. "Okay enough to help you into my bed in the next room."

"Deal." She curled her fingers around his and stood, proudly showing her body as she stepped out of the tub. "Want to hand me a towel?"

"Nope."

Gina Galvan did not blush. She didn't embarrass easily or feel self-conscious beyond her injury. Yet this man, with a hungry look and a single word, could set her on fire from the inside out.

Gina Galvan *did* know how to go after what she wanted, though. Her skin flushed with heat from head to toe. For once in her life, she felt uncomfortably warm.

While Mike's hungry perusal dappled her skin with a riot of goose bumps, that long, leanly muscled chest beckoned to her like real catnip. His attentive blue eyes told her he wanted her as much as the bulge at the front of his jeans did. She slid her arms around his waist, pressing her naked, wet body against his. She nearly lost her breath as an intense awareness sparked through every cell of her body, lighting her up from the inside out.

The tips of her breasts pebbled with the teasing caresses of his wiry chest hair and solid muscle underneath moving against her as he swept his hands down her back. He paused a moment at her waist before he curved his shoulders around her and reached lower to squeeze her bottom. The soft denim of his worn jeans stroked against her thighs as he spread his legs slightly, lifting her onto her toes and pulling her into his body. The masculine swell of his desire filled the indention between her legs and Gina pressed her face into his chest, letting her body adjust to the ribbons of heat coursing through her from every spot he touched. Matching goose bumps pricked his chest and abdomen as the cooling water dripped from her skin onto his and rivulets of moisture soaked into his jeans. Gina pressed a kiss to one chill bump, and then another, inhaling the clean scents of spicy soap and man, following a path to the firm swell of pectoral muscle. She closed her lips around the taut peak of the nipple she found there. "Now show me how bad a guy like you can be."

His muscles jerked beneath the stroke of her tongue, and Gina felt powerful, sexy, loving that he wasn't afraid to respond to her overtures. But if she thought she was in charge of this seduction, Gina was mistaken.

"Only if you promise to show me how good you can be."

Mike reached beneath her chin and tilted her face up so he could claim her mouth. He tongued the seam of her lips before thrusting between them, telling her with every stroke of the deep, drugging kiss exactly what he wanted to do with her body. Gina released his waist to wind her arms around his neck and hang on as he lapped up the droplets of water clinging to her face and neck. She willingly tipped her head back, giving his lips and tongue access to her throat and the mound of her breast before he dug his fingers into her bottom, lifted her off the floor and took the aching nipple into his mouth. Gina cried out at the fiery arrow of need that shot from the sensitive nipple deep into her core.

"Mike…" she hissed, clawing at his shoulders. She'd thought the hot, sudsy water had turned her bones to mush, but she knew if Mike let go of her now, she wouldn't be able to stand. She wrapped her legs around his waist, clinging to him as he turned his attention to the other breast. Between gasps of pleasure, she dropped kisses anyplace she could reach. The point of his chin. The strong column of his neck. She nibbled her way along the perfect line of his stubbled jaw until his hands and mouth made it impossible for her to think. "Mike… I want… Can we…?"

His lips came back to smile against her mouth and plant a kiss there. "Yes."

Despite her protests that she could walk and that she didn't want to risk aggravating his injuries by carrying her, Mike tightened his hold on her and hauled her down the hallway to his bedroom. Although he laid her gently on top of the bedspread, Gina scrambled onto her knees to maintain contact as he tossed his billfold onto the bed and shucked out of his jeans.

"I hate that you got hurt." Her fingers tangled with his, pushing the waistband of his shorts down over his leanly muscled backside. She found the ridges of scar tissue at his lower back, tracing them over his hips and partway down each thigh. Her heart constricted with compassion, then beat with admiration, over the pain he must have endured and overcome. Leaning forward, she pressed a kiss against one particularly wicked looking web of scars at the juncture of his back and hip. "I didn't fully understand how badly you'd been injured."

His skin jumped at the brush of her lips against the next scar and he turned. He grasped her by the arms and hunkered down to eye level. "This isn't pity, is it?"

"No." The intensity in those cobalt eyes was impossible to ignore. But she held that gaze, willing him to understand the depth of need and admiration she felt. "Is it for you?"

"Never." He dipped his head to kiss the newer, pinker scars on her shoulder before pushing her down on the bed and lying on the covers beside her. She trembled as he nudged his long thigh between hers to rub against that most sensitive place. He threaded his fingers into her hair and kissed her eyelids, her cheeks and the tip of her nose. "I hate that you got hurt, too. But we're not damaged goods, Gina. We're a man and a woman. Every part of me that counts is perfectly healthy. And if you can't tell how badly I want you…"

Gina pushed at his shoulders, turning him onto his back, bracing her hands against his chest, straddling his hips. "Like this?"

His answering laugh was more of a groan as she leaned over him to retrieve a condom from his billfold. His hands played with her breasts and tugged at her hair, making it difficult to concentrate on sheathing him. When his thumbs found the juncture of her thighs and pushed against her, a feverish riot of sensations bloomed like heat lightning. For a moment, she couldn't see, and her hands shook. She could barely stay upright.

Mike sat up, catching her in his arms as she tumbled into his lap. He nipped at the lobe of her ear, whispering against her skin as he lifted her slightly and slipped inside her. "Your secret is safe with me, Tiger."

"What secret?" she gasped, her body opening as he filled her, then tightening again to keep him intimately close.

He framed her face between his hands and claimed her mouth as he moved inside her. "That you're not always a tough chick. Let this happen." He kissed her again. "I've got you."

Gina nodded, believing him as she rocked over his lap in a matching rhythm that stoked the fire between them.

There were no more words. Only touches and

kisses. Gasps and moans. Strokes and shivers. The friction between them turned to passion. The teasing words became an answer to every temptation. The understanding they shared transformed into a connection that bound them closer than she'd ever been to any man. Gina had never felt so deliciously warm. She'd never felt so thoroughly loved, so completely vulnerable without feeling afraid. She buried her face in Mike's shoulder as a consuming heat blossomed in her core and seeped with delicious abandon through every part of her. She was still riding the fiery waves of pleasure when he clutched her in an almost unbearably tight embrace and found his release inside her.

Then he fell back against the pillows, pulling Gina on top of him. As she rode the deep rise and fall of his chest, he pulled the edge of the bedspread over her back, securing her against the heat of his body.

"You okay?" he whispered, feathering his fingers into her hair and tucking it gently behind her ear.

"Very okay." Gina snuggled beneath his chin. "You?"

"Very." He kissed the crown of her hair before tugging loose the other edge of the bedspread and wrapping them up in a cocoon of heat and contentment. "I'm always good when you let me get close."

Sometime later, Gina was snuggled up against Mike's chest. His arm anchored her in place as he spooned behind her. He dozed, his soft snoring stirring the wisps of hair at her neck. Gina was wide awake as darkness fell over the city. She traced the dimensions of Mike's long, agile fingers that had brought her such pleasure and ran her tongue around the abraded skin of her mouth, remembering each and every kiss they'd shared.

What was she going to do if she fell in love with Mike? How was she ever going to fit this strong, funny, brave, stubborn, generous man into her life? How could she and her needy family and demanding job be good for Mike? She wanted to be a helpmate, not a hindrance, to any man who cared about her. How would they handle children? Where could they all live without him thinking that all she wanted from him was a house with three bathrooms? What if her hand never got any better than it was right now and she couldn't return to the job she loved? What if she couldn't contribute her fair share to a relationship? Knowing Mike, he would shoulder any burden. But she didn't want to be a burden. She wanted to be his equal, the way they were right now.

She should have a plan in place for falling in love with Mike.

Because Gina knew she already had.

MIKE KNEW GINA was awake the moment he opened his eyes. Even though she was facing away from him in the bed, he could tell by the repetitive circles she traced on the back of his hand that she was deep in thought. That couldn't be a good sign.

He brushed his lips against the nape of her neck so his words wouldn't startle her. "Having regrets?"

The circles stopped. She rolled over to face him, letting him see the troubles that formed shallow lines beside her beautiful eyes. "No, but..."

"A *but* can't be good."

She patted the middle of his chest, warning him he might not like what she had to say. "Where is this leading? What kind of future can you and I have?"

Mike inhaled deeply as the familiar hints at not being good enough or no longer being necessary to a woman chafed against his ears. He wondered at the irony of his guarded sigh pushing his heart against her hand. "What kind of future do you want?"

"I have so many responsibilities. I have plans."

"And they don't include me?" He wasn't particularly proud of the bitterness that crept into his voice. But some scars were slower to heal than others. He pulled his hand from the nip of her waist and rolled onto his back. "For what it's worth, I'm not sorry we made love. I'm only sorry you can't see the possibilities between us."

She pushed herself up onto her elbows beside him. "But you can? Derek said I would sleep with you to get closer to your father and improve my chances of making SWAT."

Mike's thoughts burned with the sick idea that her partner had put into her head. "He knows he screwed up. He was lashing out at you."

"Is that why you were so quiet on the ride here? Did you think his words had hurt me?"

"I didn't like the way the Johnsons talked to you." His hand fisted over his stomach, remembering the blinding urge to ram his fist down her partner's throat for saying such hateful, untrue things. "It's one thing to hear crap like that from a stranger. But from someone you're supposed to trust?"

Gina rested her hand over his fist, willing the tension in him to relax. "I know. I thought Derek was a better man than that—a better friend. Everyone reacts differently when they feel threatened. Fight. Flight. Meanness. Fear. But in one way, he was right." She shrugged, steeling herself for some unpleasant truth she was determined to share. "There are all kinds of advantages to me being with you. But what benefit could there possibly be for you to get involved in my life?"

Mike looked up into her beautiful dark eyes. "You're kidding, right?"

She didn't think a sense of being valued, shared understandings, her great-aunt's coffee, this undeniable attraction and filling the hole in his heart were good enough reasons for a relationship? He turned his palm into hers, lacing their fingers together, trying to convey how her straightforward words and these rare glimpses of tenderness were gifts he would always treasure.

"You're Michael Cutler's son. A fine man in your own right. You have a college degree, own your own business, possess an unshakable sense of right and wrong and could have any woman you wanted." That part clearly wasn't true. But he suspected he would be even less thrilled at what she'd say next. "I grew up in No-Man's Land. I can't afford the time or money to go to college. I've got crazy stress in my life, and I'm…" her gaze shifted away to study some nameless point on the headboard as her voice trailed away "…an immigrant."

He cupped the side of her face, forcing her gaze back to his. "That's Derek and his dad talking."

Infused with a sudden energy, she rolled over and sat up, pulling the bedspread up to cover herself. "Harold Johnson called me an immigrant."

Mike sat up beside her, not understanding why the insult was something to get excited about. "He's a classless SOB. Don't let him get to you."

"He doesn't." Her animated expression told

Mike this conversation was no longer about them and their apparently lousy chance at a future. "That's another way all the cop shootings are connected. Colin Cho. Frank McBride. Gina Galvan. Other than Derek, the victims have all been minority cops." She tilted her gaze to his. "Is that a coincidence?"

He shifted gears back to work with her. "Or a sad statement about some of our world today." Apparently, the discussion about a future together had ended.

"So many possible motives. So many reasons one person would want to hurt so many others." When she linked her arm through his and rested her cheek against his shoulder, the edgy frustration he'd felt a moment earlier abated. "Mike?"

"Hmm?"

"I'm sorry I called you *Choir Boy*. That probably didn't feel any different than Harold or Bobby Etes or the Bismarcks calling me *chica* or *querida*. They're labels. Assumptions. Even in jest, those nicknames show a lack of respect. Men like that—they don't care enough to get to know me. I don't want you to think I feel that same way about you. I'm sorry."

He turned his head to kiss her temple. "Apology accepted."

Her soft, lyrical laugh vibrated against his skin. "You *are* too nice."

Mike was beginning to think that there could

be a way for the two of them to make this work, when Gina's phone rang.

"Sorry," she apologized, pulling away. "Hazard of the job."

But she got tangled in the covers. Mike pulled the quilt up to her neck and motioned for her to stay put, while he slipped out of bed. "I grew up with Michael Cutler. I understand interruptions. Dinners. Football games. Driving lessons." He grabbed his jeans and jogged down the hall to retrieve her phone from the guest bathroom. She followed right behind him, two silly grown-ups running naked through his house.

When he handed her the phone, Gina saw the number and frowned. "Hazard of my family," she corrected. She offered him a silent apology as she swiped the answer icon. "*Hola?* This is Gina."

Since he couldn't understand the frantic, high-pitched tones, he assumed the caller was speaking in Spanish. But there was no second-guessing the color draining from Gina's olive skin. Before Mike could ask what was wrong, she was moving, grabbing her clothes, sliding into her shoes, putting on that tough-chick armor that couldn't quite mask the stark fear in her eyes. "Call 9-1-1. Is anyone hurt?" She was visibly shaking by the time she responded to the answer. "Tell them to send an ambulance. Lock the doors, and stay inside. Stay away from the windows. I'm on my way."

Mike had already pulled on his shorts and jeans by the time the conversation had ended. "What's happened?"

Gina reached for his hand, holding on tightly, pulling him toward the front door. "Someone shot up my aunt and uncle's house."

Chapter Thirteen

For the second time in as many days, Gina raced across Kansas City with Mike at the wheel.

An ambulance was already pulling away from the scene by the time Mike screeched to a stop at the end of the block. Gina was already on the ground and running before the truck stopped rocking. *"Mami! Papi!"* She spotted her brother and sister just outside a strip of yellow crime scene tape, wrapping up a conversation with Detective Grove. The overbuilt detective thanked them and moved away to take a phone call. "Javi? Sylvie? What happened? Who's hurt? Is this Bobby's doing?"

"Whoa!" Javier caught her briefly against his stocky chest before she turned away to hug Sylvie. But Mike had followed right at her heels, and now Sylvie was attached to his waist, wrapped up in a brotherly hug. "Nobody got shot, sis. We were all back in the kitchen eating dinner. We heard the gunshots and dove for the floor."

She glanced over at the bullet-ridden front porch and shattered windows at the front of the house. "But the ambulance?"

Javier tightened his arm around her shoulders. "It's Tio Papi. He had a heart attack."

Gina's stomach fell. "Is he…?"

Suddenly, she felt Mike's warm hand slide beneath the curls at the nape of her neck. His tone was as grounding as his touch. "Let's get the facts before we react to anything."

Sylvie pulled away from the anchor of Mike's chest and sniffed back the tears she'd been crying. "The paramedics said he was alert and responsive."

"That's a good sign," Mike agreed.

Sylvie nodded. "He was so pale. He couldn't catch his breath. I gave him a baby aspirin, just like the 9-1-1 lady said."

Mike kept Sylvie turned away from the officers securing the chaotic scene. The CSI van had arrived, too, and the techs were gearing up to remove bullets and analyze any usable foot prints or tire tracks. Kevin Grove was still on his phone, while his partner directed two other officers to close off either end of the block with their cruisers. Neighbors were at their windows or peeking out front doors, too afraid to step out into the night.

"Good girl," Mike praised Sylvie. Gina appreciated that he was keeping her siblings calm and focused, while she was a roiling mass of suspicion and fear and protective anger. "A stressor like having his home attacked could certainly cause it. Are they taking him to St. Luke's?"

The nearest hospital made sense. Javier nodded. "I was just about to drive over there with Sylvie. They look Tia Lupe in the ambulance, too, to monitor her blood pressure, they said. She was sitting up."

"That's standard precautionary procedure once you reach a certain age," Mike said. "It's good for both of them to be together at a time like this." He clapped Javier on the shoulder. "It'll be even better once they're surrounded by their family. You two go on. We'll meet you there later."

Javier frowned at Gina. "You're not coming with us?"

Gina had only been half listening to the conversation. Her attention had shifted to the flashing lights of a criminologist snapping photo after photo of the bullet holes in the posts and siding and chipped bricks on the front porch. And to Detective Grove's clipped conversation that included words like *Bismarck* and *BOLO* or Be On the Lookout For. On the lookout for who?

"I think your sister is in cop mode right now." She was. Mike told Javier and Sylvie to call them as soon as they learned more about their great-aunt and -uncle, then shooed them toward the car. "Don't worry. I'll stay with her. We'll be there as soon as we can."

By the time Javier and Sylvie had taken off, Gina had done a complete 360. Every cell in her body was screaming on high alert. The street and yards were already crowded with cars and junk. There were too many people here. Too many distractions. Too many places to hide. "This is a setup. This whole thing is a trap." The moment Kevin Grove hung up the phone, she ducked beneath the crime scene tape and marched over to him. "Detective Grove? You need to get your men out of here."

He didn't seem fazed that she'd entered the crime scene without permission. "This is the home of a cop, Galvan. Another attempted murder. Of you."

Gina shook her head. "No one was shot here. Not yet." She could feel the truth in her bones as clearly as if she was reading the information off a computer screen. "Have you recovered any of the bullets yet?"

The detective pulled a plastic evidence bag from his pocket for her to examine.

"These aren't like the bullets we took from Bobby Estes. These are rifle caliber."

"Estes carries a hand gun?"

Gina nodded as he pocketed the slugs. "The shooter is here. I know it. This is exactly the kind of chaos he thrives on. The perfect cover. While you and your people are focused on doing their jobs, he's picking out his target." She scanned the chaos and shadows around them. "Whoever he's after this time, he already has them in his sights."

Kevin Grove might be as stubborn as they came, but he was one of the best detectives in all of KCPD. He listened to Gina's take on the situation and started shouting orders. "I want a car-to-car search of anything parked within targeting distance. Clear all nonessential personnel out of here. Everyone on the scene wears a flak vest." He pointed to the porch lights across the street. "Let's get these civilians away from the windows and kill some of these lights. I don't want this guy having any advantage we don't." After the uniformed officers and CSIs scrambled away to do his bidding, Detective Grove looked down at Gina. "You got your badge on you? We can use every available cop right now."

"She's ready." Gina turned to see Mike holding out her badge and holstered Glock that she'd stowed in his truck. His half grin belied the serious warning in his eyes. "I figured you were going to jump into the middle of this, even if you are still on medical leave. I'd rather have you armed and able to defend yourself than be a sitting duck."

"Works for me." Grove nodded toward one of the officers jogging to the house next door. "Since you know these people, why don't you make the rounds and warn your neighbors to keep their heads down until we're finished."

"Yes, sir." Gina took the badge and gun and slipped them onto her belt. Mike's understanding of who she was touched her. Strapping the Glock onto her hip for the first time in almost two months was both empowering—like putting on a favorite pair of jeans—and a little unnerving. This wasn't just a good luck charm she was wearing. It was a loaded lethal weapon. And she was responsible for her use of it.

"You can do this, Tiger." She tilted her gaze up to those piercing blue eyes. Mike Cutler believed in her. So she believed, too. When Gina nodded, Mike reached for her damaged hand and squeezed, reminding her that she could feel with those fingers, she could control her body. She could do this.

She quickly squeezed back. "Thank you."

"Let's go."

"Go? Where are you going?" she chided, hurrying her steps to catch up with his long stride. "Not a cop, Cutler. You need to go back to your truck and get out of here."

But once she slipped under the crime scene tape he held up for her, he fell into step right beside her. "We're partners, remember?"

"Not when it comes to something this dangerous."

"You're not getting rid of me," he insisted.

"Fine. Just keep up."

Gina coordinated the contact with and notification to the residents of the nearby houses with the other officer, taking the east end of the block. She knocked on the doors of two houses, asking the residents if they'd seen anything, then warning them back into interior rooms of the house until KCPD had fully cleared the scene.

She'd just headed up the next front walk when Mike stopped at the edge of the driveway. "Gina."

She followed the general direction of his gaze to the north–south side street. A familiar tan Mercedes cruised slowly through the intersection. The driver watched the police cars blocking the street and the officers still moving around her great-uncle's house.

"That's your stolen license plate."

She spotted the last two digits, 3-6, as the car passed beneath the glow of the streetlamp at the corner. A shiver ran down her spine. Along with a sense of finality and purpose.

Mike was already moving toward the slow-moving vehicle when she joined him. "That's Bobby Estes." What was he doing here? Could he have something to do with the attack on her family, after all? It wouldn't be that hard for him or one of his friends to get a different weapon. Gina tossed Mike her phone as she quickened her pace to keep the car in sight. "Detective Grove's number is in there. Call him and let him know. I'll track the car as long as I can."

By the time Gina reached the corner, Bobby picked up speed. She ran across the street, chasing him past Mike's truck and down the sidewalk to the next intersection. But Bobby gunned the powerful engine and careened out of sight, leaving her no chance of catching him on foot. She stopped at the curb, breathing hard at the full-out sprint, her mouth open, her nostrils flaring. Her only hope was that Mike had gotten through to Detective Grove and an APB on the car and license would stop him before he got too far away. "You son of a…"

As her breathing eased and the urge to curse faded, Gina realized that she'd just run past a piece-of-junk Chevy. She let go of her enmity toward Bobby Estes as a chilling suspicion took its place.

Piece-of-junk Chevy. Derek's particular choice of words rang in her ears. He *had* remembered something from the day of the shooting. Gina slowly turned as the ghost of a forgotten image filled her head. There. A dented 1500 pickup with a faded red side panel and rusted wheel wells was parked up the street, lost among the bumper-to-bumper heaps that littered the neighborhood. It was far enough away from her house not to be caught in the grid of police officers blocking out a crime scene, but it sat at an angle that gave its driver a clear view of everything happening along the street. Its unremarkable appearance had camouflaged it from notice. But she saw it now. Saw it clearly. She took one step toward it. Two. She saw the tip of the rifle balanced through the open window. Aimed right at her.

"Gun!" Gina yelled a split second before she saw the flash of gunpowder lighting up the night.

The boom of the big gun's report hit her a nanosecond later. Before she could react, a long, broad chest slammed into her, tackling her to the ground. Mike. Of course. Rescuing her. Again.

She heard a rare curse against her ear. A second gunshot split the air. With his long arms snaked around her, they rolled, scraping across the unforgiving concrete before they hit crinkly brown grass and slammed to a stop against a fire hydrant. Mike's back took the brunt of the impact, and he swore again.

"Mike! Are you hurt?"

But he was pushing her out of his arms. An engine roared to life in the distance. He pushed her to her feet as he sat up. "Go!" Tires squealing against the pavement, fighting for traction, drowned out the engine noise. Mike shoved her away from him. "Go get him!"

Gina shook off the dizziness from their tumble and started moving. By the time she saw the other officers running toward the intersection, the Chevy had already bashed in the bumper of the car in front of it and was flying down the street. He was getting away. He couldn't get away.

Gina unhooked her holster and stepped into the middle of the street.

"Gina!"

"KCPD!" she shouted. "Stop the car!" She pulled out her Glock. "Stop the car!"

It picked up speed and raced toward her in a deadly game of chicken. No more wounded cops. This guy wasn't winning. Not on her turf.

Gina raised the gun with both hands, willed her shaky fingers to be strong, slid her finger against the trigger. "Stop the damn car!"

When the driver answered by gunning the engine, Gina squeezed the trigger. She felt the kick in her shoulder and steadied her aim, firing again and again. She took out one headlight, shattered the windshield, popped a tire and kept firing until the truck spun out of control and crashed into a row of parked cars.

The other officers were on the scene in an instant. Kevin Grove pulled the driver out of the car and put him down on the ground, cuffing him. Several other officers had rushed in to turn off the Chevy's motor and assist Grove with dragging him up onto the sidewalk before Gina reached the wreck.

Gina's hand, still holding the gun, was shaking

down at her side. She recognized the oily gray ponytail and interrupted the detective charging the perp with numerous crimes. "Harold? Harold Johnson?"

"I didn't kill anybody," Derek's father protested, spitting his anger at everyone around him. "I didn't kill anybody. You can't get me for murder."

Gina shook her head. The adrenaline that had charged through her system a moment ago was draining away, leaving her stunned by the discovery of the man who'd hurt her. "You shot four cops. You shot your own son."

"That was a decoy. A flesh wound. I knew he'd recover. You were the one I was aiming for. Maimed you good, didn't I? Turned you into a cripple."

"You son of a…"

She startled at Mike's touch on her arm, urging her to holster her weapon. "Why?" he asked. "What do you get out of this?"

"It's what Derek gets. What my boy deserves." Gina still didn't understand. "They were going to promote you and that—"

"Shut up, Johnson," Mike warned.

"—ahead of my boy. You immigrants don't deserve a better job. You get special treatment you haven't earned. Just because your skin's a different color or you got boobs instead of—"

"He said to shut up." Grove dragged him to his

feet. "Did Derek know about this? Know how you were stacking the odds in his favor?"

"Not at first. But he figured it out." He pointed his nose at Gina since his hands were bound. "Because of all that poking around that you were doing, he figured it out. He knows where his loyalties are. Unlike his lousy partner, who files complaints on him." Harold's face had been cut by some broken glass. His cheek was already swelling from where he must have smacked into the window or steering wheel when he crashed. But his injuries didn't stop him from spewing his vile prejudice. "I screwed up a lot in Derek's life, but I could do this for him. Made it so you couldn't be a cop no more. I got rid of the competition." He snorted a curse. "I thought you couldn't handle a gun no more."

Gina looked right into those bloodshot green eyes without blinking. "I got better."

"Someone take this jackass off my hands. I want to see Officer Johnson at my desk before the night's over," Detective Grove ordered. "Call Impound. And let's contain this scene." While others hurried to carry out his orders, the burly detective smiled down at Gina. "Good work, Galvan. Welcome back. I'd put you on my team any day. I'll get a report from you later." Then he nodded up to Mike. "In the meantime, you'd better get him to the hospital."

"What? Mike!" Gina spun around. Mike was

holding on to his left bicep and blood was oozing between his fingers. More than the shock of learning the identity of the man who'd shot her, more than the disappointment of knowing Derek had hidden the truth from her, seeing Mike bleeding because of her might be the one thing she couldn't handle. "You need to sit down." She slipped her arm around his waist and started walking toward his truck. "What were you thinking?"

"That you are the most magnificent woman I've ever known. Facing Johnson down like that."

"I don't mean that. Harold was shooting at *me*. At cops."

"I didn't want you to get hurt."

"It's not okay for you to get hurt, either."

"It's just a graze. A few stitches and a shot of antibiotics and I'll be good."

Even though he seemed to be walking fine under his own power, Gina kept a steadying arm around him. Maybe she was steadying herself because her vision was blurring and her heart was breaking and she couldn't stand that she was falling apart. He sat on the running board of the truck, while she rummaged beneath the front seat to find his first aid kit.

When she knelt in front of him, he captured the side of her face in his hand and wiped away the tears with the pad of his thumb. "Hey. What are these? I didn't think tough chicks cried."

She unbuttoned his shirt and gently peeled the cotton sleeve off his shoulder and away from the wound. "I hate you, Michael Cutler Jr. I hate you for making me cry."

"Um, okay?"

She dabbed at the blood with a wad of gauze, relieved to see it was just a flesh wound. "I'm crying because you're hurt and I'm in love with you."

"You're not selling me on this, Tiger." He pulled her hand away from stanching his wound and dipped his head to meet her gaze. "Does it help if I tell you I'm in love with you, too?"

"You are?" The man had such incredibly blue eyes.

"Has there been one moment when you doubted that I cared about you?"

Gina stretched up to press a hard kiss against his mouth. When she pulled away, his lips followed hers to claim another kiss. Then she caught his stubbled jaw in her hand and kissed him again, feeling the fear fading and the emotional strength this man inspired in her returning. "I don't know yet how we're going to make this work. But we are going to make it work. Understand? You know how good I am at fighting for what I want."

"Do you mind if I fight for us, too?"

"But no more jumping in front of bullets, okay? No more running down bad guys." She poked a finger in the middle of his chest. "Not a cop. Even if I don't make SWAT, I'm going back to a beat or working with domestic-violence victims or earning my detective's badge. That's my job."

"If we're going to be a partnership, what is my job?"

Those blue eyes mesmerized her. Treasured her. Believed in her. "To love me every day of your long and healthy life."

Mike wound his uninjured arm around her and pulled her in for a kiss. "Deal."

Epilogue

Two months later

Mike would never tire of seeing Gina in her starched KCPD uniform. She walked into the CAPT clinic with takeout and drinks to share lunch in his office and his heart did a familiar tumble of love and pride. She carried herself with confidence when she wore the blue-and-black with her badge, gear belt and holstered gun. And her sweet figure filled it out in a way that was anything but mannish.

He waited while she greeted Troy and leaned in to give him a hug. Mike dutifully raised his gaze to her dark eyes when she turned to include him in her announcement. "Did I tell you I've already got three people signed up to take my self-defense training class here? Vicki Bismarck, Frannie and Sylvie. Lupe said she's going to bake cookies and bring them down to watch. Says maybe she's not so old that she can't learn a thing or two."

"Lupe's baking cookies?" Troy raised his hand. "Anything I can do to help with your class?" When Mike and Gina laughed, Troy pressed his hand against his heart. "Hey, I'm serious. She's brought food to each of the sessions where I've been helping her work on her balance issues."

Mike took the bag from Gina before teasing his friend. "You know that's not how we get our bills paid around here, right?"

"Yeah, but don't tell her that. That woman can cook."

Although Gina smiled much more often these days, she was serious for a moment. "So, it's okay if I set up my class here? I know it's not physical therapy, but you are in the neighborhood."

Mike read the agreement on Troy's face and nodded. "I think feeling safe and building self-confidence all fits into that wellness goal we strive for. Just let me know when and I'll schedule the gym for you."

Frannie came out of her office carrying a computer pad. "As long as you leave Monday and Wednesday nights open. That's when Colin Cho and Frank McBride are coming in for their PT."

Mike couldn't deny the recent upturn in business. Or the credit Gina deserved for helping him. "I wouldn't have thought you'd be the best PR person. But you've brought in a half dozen new clients from KCPD."

Gina shrugged. "Cops have a lot of back and joint issues. I just suggested they come here."

Troy rolled his chair up beside Frannie. "Hey, you signed up for Gina's class? You gonna wear those tight shorts you had on the last time you worked out?"

"Troy!" Her freckles disappeared beneath a healthy blush.

"Like I'm not gonna notice." Troy grabbed Frannie around the waist and pulled her into his lap before wheeling them both into the gym. "C'mon, Sunshine. Let's get you warmed up."

Once they were alone in the hallway, Gina smiled. "They seem happy."

"They do." Mike led her into his office and set lunch out on his desk while Gina closed the door. "What about you, Tiger? Are you happy?"

"What do you think?" Gina was right there when he faced her. She nudged him onto the edge of the desk, moved between his legs and kissed him very, very thoroughly.

Mike returned the favor, pulling her onto her toes and taking over the kiss. When she mewled that telltale hum in her throat that told him they were about to take this embrace past the point of no return, Mike set her back on her feet. He settled his hands at her waist, resting his forehead against hers as they both struggled to return their breathing to normal. "Do you like working the special victims unit? I know how badly you wanted SWAT."

"There'll be other SWAT teams. The guys who made it deserve the honor." She tilted her gaze up to his, sharing an honest, beautiful smile. "Maybe one day my shoulder will be good enough so I can make the cut. If not, I'm okay. I think I'm really good at what I'm doing now."

"You'd be good at anything you set your mind to."

"Your dad doesn't still feel guilty about not putting me on the new SWAT team, does he?"

"No. I think he's happier to know he's got you for a future daughter-in-law."

Resting her hand against his chest, Gina eyed the simple solitaire he'd given her. "Me, too."

They shared another kiss before sitting down to lunch. As it often did between them, the conversation turned to her work and family. By the time they'd finished, she'd updated him on the Bismarck brothers, who were both in jail now. Rollo Molina's health was still a concern, but his stress was more manageable now that Mike had moved the family into his home. Lupe cooked, Javier helped with the yard and Gina had planted a garden. Bobby Estes was still trading favors for fast cars in No-Man's Land, but at least he'd stopped pestering Sylvie. "We'll have to catch him at something where we can make the arrest stick," Gina groused. "But I like a project."

"Just say the word and I will help you do whatever is necessary to get Estes off the streets." Mike stood as Gina circled the desk to meet him.

"Not a cop, Cutler."

"No, but *you* are, Gina Galvan." He leaned in to kiss the teasing reminder off her mouth. "You're my cop."

* * * * *

Get 2 Free Books,
Plus 2 Free Gifts—
just for trying the
Reader Service!

Get 2 Free Books,
Plus 2 Free Gifts—
just for trying the Reader Service!

Get 2 Free Books,
<u>Plus</u> 2 Free Gifts -
just for trying the *Reader Service!*